TO THE BOTTOM
OF THE HELL-CITY

I saw the floater, poised in mid-air in the shaft. I leaped toward it and landed precariously on the tiny tongue-board below the door—an infinity of darkness below me.

"Jeremy," I hear her shout through the walls of the ship, and then her face was at the door. We looked at each other through that cruel glass for seconds.

Then the man the Undergrounders called Mister President came up beside her; for an instant his pale, great-eyed face was beside hers in a hideous cameo—and then he pulled a lever, and the tongue-board scraped into the side of the ship.

At first the fall was slow, almost leisurely. I remember looking up and seeing the running-lights of the floater moving in slow, tight circles as I plummetted down, down, down...

WOLFHEAD

CHARLES L. HARNESS

A BERKLEY MEDALLION BOOK
published by
BERKLEY PUBLISHING CORPORATION

Berkley Publishing Corporation
200 Madison Avenue
New York, N.Y. 10016

SBN 425-03658-8

BERKLEY MEDALLION BOOKS are published by
Berkley Publishing Corporation
200 Madison Avenue
New York, N. Y. 10016

BERKLEY MEDALLION BOOK ® TM 757,375

Printed in the United States of America

Berkley Medallion Edition, FEBRUARY, 1978

PROLOGUE

Now came a she wolf, lean and horrid.
She has brought (and she will bring)
Many to grief.
> The Prophet Dante, *Inferno*, Canto I.

Day fades to evening; the darkening air
releases all creatures from their daily tasks,
   save me.
For I must make ready for my great journey.
The death and blood and pity that I met,
my memory shall now retrace.
> The Prophet Dante, *Inferno*, Canto II.

Like the great prophet, I write this because
I must.

I think of them all, men, women, children.
Innocents, nearly all of them. We bore each
other no ill will. Most of them did not even
know I existed. In my nightmares I see their
strange white faces. I waken, sweating.

I write this so that the thing may be finally
finished.

Was It Hours, or Years Ago?
All through the sunlit fields we ran.
We trod the shady forest trails.
I felt your face, I touched your hand.
We wandered wide o'er hill and vale.

Everywhere, Nowhere
I see you in the clouds that fly
In fleecy lines across the sky.
Your whispers mingle with the leaves
That drift from autumn's changeling trees.

I Wake, and Listen
In the darkness of my cabin
I hear a step. I call a name.
Is it but the wind, tapping,
Sighing at my windowpane?

1. WHO I AM

MY NAME IS Jeremy Wolfhead. Actually, I don't have a wolf head. For better or worse, it is a rather ordinary head, with yellow hair and blue eyes. Grandfather used to say that even if I had the intelligence of a dire wolf, I still wouldn't be smart enough to take over the business after he dies. (Wolfhead and Company, Restorations.)

Our family has been called Wolfhead as far back as the records go. There are two theories as to how we got the name. Firstly, perhaps one of my ancestors really had a wolf head, and became famous for it, and so started our name. If so, he was born in the days of the Desolation, when such mutations were commonplace, perhaps even a source of pride, and not a subject for dismay as they are today. The second explanation is perhaps closer to the mark. Many centuries ago one of my ancestors, a Friar named Cornhunter, prophesied that one of our family would take the head of a wolf, descend into hell, destroy a great and evil culture, and come out safe again. Traditionally our family smiled at Brother Cornhunter, and some of our wiser people thought him quite mad.

1

The strange psychic powers of the Friars (also called the Brothers) are now much lessened, and perhaps I am the cause of it, for better or worse. I don't believe the loss matters much. The Brothers emerged, some two thousand years ago, to guide and succor what was left of us, and to preserve some of our crumbled civilization. They taught us how to plant, how to raise livestock, and to read and write. From them we relearned metallurgy and our simple sciences. They kept the healing arts to themselves, but the rest they taught well, and they will be remembered forever for it.

My ancestors originally lived on the banks of the great Mispi River. Three hundred years ago (so our tradition goes) one of them, Messer Fallowt Wolfhead, gathered up his wife, children, horses, and cattle, and began the trek east. He had heard (from the friars, probably) that the radiation left over from the Desolation had waned and was no longer lethal, and that the land was rich and fertile again. It took his wagons four months to make the journey, for there were no roads then, and no air machines. (It would be another two hundred years before his descendants dug the first floater out of the debris of the suburbs of ancient Freddrick and restored it.)

Having arrived at the Lantick Ocean (which quite astonished my ancestor), he scouted the shore for one hundred miles in either direction and finally selected what is now called Horseshoe Bay. This is a cliff-lined circle of water about ten miles in diameter facing squarely on the ocean. The eastern seaboard is peppered with hundreds of these giant circles, some larger, some smaller. Sometimes they seem to merge together to make one colossal pit, which is generally full of water and makes a fine lake. For example, to the southwest of us there is a very large lake having numerous scalloped edges. This very beautiful lake stands (if you will believe our teaching Friars) where the ancient city of Washton once stood.

Horseshoe Bay bites deep into the shore, and at its deepest recess, the land dips down to the water, making an excellent harbor. Most any day you can stand on the rim and watch the ships. You will see both sailing ships and the faster nuclear vessels (many restored by grandfather's shops). The land all around the horseshoe is flat and fertile. It is watered by several streams, and rainfall is plentiful. So here my forefathers settled. Other immigrants from the west joined them. Over the years, farms became villages, some of the villages became towns, and the town at the harbor became New Bollamer.

During this time contact with other peoples in other lands, even across the great Lantick, was reestablished.

When my ancestors settled here, they were under the very reasonable impression that they were the only human beings within hundreds of miles.

I will tell you now (so that we can dispose of the matter and get on to other things), I like to hunt. My grandfather taught me when I was a boy. I kept it up when I entered Bollamer Collegia to begin my study of Excavation and Restoration. I very nearly did not graduate because I got fed up during the middle of exam week and took the floater up into the Penn Woods in search of a giant stag I had heard about. Armed only with a good hunting knife, I followed the stag south on foot for four days and four nights, with no rest for him or for me. He tried to escape me by swimming nearly a mile across a very cold lake. But I was right behind him. (I dearly love a good swim.)

Soon after we emerged from the lake the scenery began to change.

Overhead I noticed low fog clouds, sweeping eastward over the tree tops, and I heard a dull thunder, growing louder in the west. I suddenly realized where we were. This splendid animal was leading me to the

Spume, where he might lose his pursuer in the ground wraiths, scentless steam, and deafening noise that accompanied this remarkable phenomenon. It was his final effort to stay alive. And indeed it was an immensely clever and desperate thing for an animal to come here, over so many miles, to engineer his final attempt at escape. As far as I was concerned, he had earned his life, and I then and there gave it back to him.

I knew the Spume only by reputation. This was my first actual confrontation, and I was eager to see it. In moments I was at the top of the hill and looking over at the colossus. I could see and hear the whole thing.

The Spume crater had been built up over the course of centuries as a drenched and mottled cone of jumbled rocks, a hundred yards across from lip to lip. A column of steam roared two miles skyward out of this crater. For a circle a mile around, there were only a couple of trees, and these were dead. The area was grief stricken, desolate.

Only the Spume was alive.

As I stood there, entranced, a great rock broke off from the crater edge and fell into the steam column. It must have been half as large as our stable; yet it was hurled up and out again immediately, and it crashed a thousand yards away from me on the other side of the crater. Despite the distance, I felt the earth shake beneath my feet.

But all of this was simply the framework, the physical setting, as it were, for the mighty thing that was taking place there, continuously, hour by hour, day by day, and century by century. My neck arched back as, with unbelieving eyes, I followed the steam column upward. When the steam finally ceased to rise any higher, the top layer began to float eastward with the prevailing wind. And then, far at the top of that magnificent plume, the steam began to change, mostly, I think, on account of the cold. (For it was mid-January.) The steam first condensed to water droplets.

Some of these fell as rain, within the barren annihilated area. Some water droplets were exposed longer to the cold, and these fell as sleet and hail. Some joined together to make ice stones big enough to break a man's skull. I jumped as a fist-sized ball of ice fell almost at my feet. Getting my head broken would be a silly way to end a great hunt, so I retreated a hundred yards up the hill. There I saw another remarkable thing. Off to my right was a strange white mountain, which I judged to be made entirely of snow. Some of the steam was changing to snow, and it was falling from great heights and with great whispering hisses, to make a long, dune-shaped drift, perhaps half a mile high and a mile wide, and stretching out eastward for miles and miles, over the forest, at the beck of the west wind.

While I was standing spellbound I noticed movement below. The great stag skirted the deadly bombardment of ice, circled the deafening steam column, and disappeared on the other side. Three dire wolves were running close behind him. He would probably die deaf, and the wolves might never hear properly again. What a sorry end to four days and nights on the trail! I held my hands over my head, closed my eyes to slits, and, keeping a safe distance from the Spume, ran in a great circle to follow them.

There on the other side of the vapor pillar, I found them. The antlered king had been pulled down by the wolves, who were even now, amid steam, sleet, noise, and snowfall, eating him alive. One wolf lifted his head in my direction, snarled, and started for me. Fortunately there was a great dead tree nearby. I shinnied up that trunk inches ahead of clicking teeth. As I climbed I cursed my decision to bring a knife instead of a rifle. But even with a rifle, it would have been stupid to try to sneak away with night about to fall, because, although I could not see the wolves, they could see me very well indeed. And I will now explain why this is so.

The Brothers tell us that during the centuries of the Desolation, immense clouds of dust covered the skies, blotting out the sun, giving an eternal night. Certain strange plants and animals developed that could cope better with the darkness. The dire wolf was one. It can "see" in total blackness by means of infra-red sensors in its ocular cavities. So for nocturnal operations these animals had a tremendous advantage over a mere human being.

A final observation. From the crotch of branches where I spent the night, I had to dislodge the rib cage of some strange vertebrate, long ago picked clean by crows and buzzards. How it had got up into the tree I could not then imagine. (I learned only much later.) And so I spent an uncomfortable night, shivering, and pondering the awesome power of the Spume and the contrary nature of dire wolves.

The next week I was back at the collegia. Grandfather had to finance a chair of Nuclear Engine Rebuilding, and then they let me graduate.

Afterwards, when I was working in Grandfather's shops, I often thought about that gorgeous prince of antlers. He stood over seven feet at the shoulder. I am only five feet ten inches, and a mere fraction of his weight, yet I persisted. I do not know anyone who has run down a giant stag. As long as he had to get eaten, I would rather we did it, and not the wolves. So, in a way, I was sorry I could not get him home into our food locker. Not that Grandfather likes venison. But he buys it when the hunters bring it around. And you will find heads of giant stags in his trophy room at the lodge. He shot them all himself, when he was a young man. But he can no longer take the time, he claims, especially since he has to give my work such careful supervision and make sure he catches all my mistakes. As otherwise (he says) my visi sets seem to turn into radios and my atom engines run backward. Actually, I was not all that bad, but I did tend to think about hunting a lot, even when I should have been finishing a restoration.

At this point perhaps I should explain what happened to my parents.

They are dead.

One fine morning (and fresh from the wedding bed, for he had married my mother but the week before) my father set off jauntily in his little floater, *Wolfhead*, with the avowed purpose of exploring the sea caves along the coast. He sailed out over the bay, with my mother waving to him merrily, and he disappeared around the cliffs, and neither he nor *Wolfhead* was ever seen again. My mother died in childbirth, partly from an infection following my entry into the world and partly because she could not accept the fact that my father was dead. And so my grandfather took over my upbringing.

2. BEATRA

I MET BEATRA at the Winter Ball. The orchestra was still
tuning up, and the actual dancing had not yet begun.
Floaters were still arriving. Most of the men were in the
wineroom. The upstairs dressing room was full of
ladies. And that is where the action started.

I well remember. I had just entered the lobby, and
was in the act of handing my greatcoat to the footman,
when the Lady Mary Weaver burst out upon the
upstairs landing, shrieking and waving her arms. I was
first to cross the dance floor and to bound up the stairs
to her rescue.

"In there!" She did not need to point. Girls, ladies,
dames, females of all ages and in various stages of
finery were pouring out of the room.

"What is it?" I demanded.

But not one of them would answer me. They were
too terrified to speak.

Evidently a dangerous animal had crawled up the
guttering, broken into the window, and even now was
preparing to come forth and attack these helpless

creatures! Perhaps a giant carcajou, teeth bared and slavering, was even now slinking toward the door!

I had no weapon. I turned to the men by me. "An electro? A knife? Anything?"

They shook their heads.

There was an empty suit of armour at the top of the stairs. The empty metal glove held a great pikestaff. I wrenched it away and strode to the door.

"Careful, man," cried voices behind me.

I held the staff high like a spear and leaped inside. There was a flash of movement to my right. I very nearly hurled the staff. And then when I saw what caused the movement, I felt faint.

It was a girl. A very beautiful girl. She was standing before a mirror, and she had been in the simple act of pulling her slip down over her body. I caught a glimpse of bare thighs, of thinly concealed legs and belly.

I looked around the room quickly. There was no beast. There was nothing.

The stained glass window was open by half an inch. "Did it go back down the gutter?" I asked, without looking at her.

"No, milord, it didn't go back down the gutter." She was now struggling to pull her gown down over her head. "I need help."

"But . . . the *animal* . . . ?"

"It is under the wardrobe cabinet."

The cabinet sat barely an inch off the floor. Now I understood. I dropped the halberd and went over to help her. "A mouse?"

"A mouse. Now, you must pull down, on both sides, and then there are certain catches and buttons."

I did everything just the way she instructed. I felt her soft flesh through the folds of cloth. Not that I was trying to. I smelled her perfume, a light, delicate thing, like wild cherry pollen in early morning.

"Thank you, kind sir," she said, looking at herself in the mirror from all angles. "Now, about our little visitor. I shall pass the handle of your staff under the wardrobe, and when Sir Grayfur runs out, you must slap your kerchief down over him."

"Couldn't I just jump on him?"

"Certainly not!" Without a backward glance, she walked over to the wardrobe with the heavy staff.

She had made it sound easy. But it wasn't. It took several tries, because the little creature zigzagged quite a bit. But finally I had him wrapped in my best blue kerchief.

I looked at her. "What now?"

"Drop him out the window."

I objected. "The fall won't kill him. It is barely twenty feet, and there is six inches of soft snow on the ground."

"Exactly."

And so I did.

"Now give me your kerchief." She took it to the backroom and washed it out. "You can pick it up some time..."

Oh, she was beautiful! I said, "Since you are now adequately rescued, may I have the first dance?"

"I would be honored, O mighty hunter." She curtsied deep, then took my arm. We walked through the throng at the doorway, leaving the halberd on the floor, and let them make their wildest surmises.

Six weeks later Beatra and I were married and living at Horseshoe Manor.

3. KIDNAPPED

WE HAD BEEN married a matter of days, when we both took a notion to arise very early on a certain morning in an attempt to view a strange phenomenon known as the "gods-eye." This was a brilliant, starlike pinpoint of light, visible best early in the morning or in late evening, which arced briefly across the sky and then vanished.

The tiny bell sounded. I was already nearly awake, and I reached over and turned off the alarm. I looked briefly at the illuminated numbers on the chron: 5:30.

It was totally dark, and I could not make out Beatra's form under the furs beside me. But she was there. Ah, she was there...

In the dark I heard the great hound scramble to his feet. "Not a sound, Goro," I whispered. "Be a good fellow, and in a moment we will all go for a walk." I heard a muffled whine and the swish of the tail wagging.

I eased out of bed, found my sandals and robe, and shuffled over to the massive shuttered windows. They groaned as I pulled them back. I peered through the iron gratings and beyond the cliff to the water. Horseshoe Bay reflected the stars like a mirror. The sky was clear. No moon. No clouds. I stared hard toward the northeast. Nothing there yet. Good. I looked down into the statuary garden. Nothing stirred the cedars. Off to the left and right, and barely visible, were the edges of the orchards and cornfields, dark and somnolent. All was as it should be. We were an hour to cockcrow.

I returned to the bed. Beatra was still asleep.

And now I hesitated a moment. Perhaps owing to the chill, perhaps due to a sudden horrid premonition, I shivered. Here was the fork in the path that the Brothers mention, one way leading to success and safety, the other to total disaster. It was our last chance. But (as I so well remember) all I could think of then was proceeding with our plan for the hour. I leaned over and ran my hand over the outline of her body and came to rest on her bare neck. She awoke drowsily.

"I'm going to turn on the porto-lamp," I said.

She groaned sleepily. "What time is it?"

"Time to get up. The awakener has sounded."

She pushed the great bearskin back and sat up in bed. "The honeymoon is over. Married two weeks, and now roused from bed in the middle of the night."

"It's five-thirty, going on six."

"It is pitch dark and it is the middle of the night."

"Come look out the window. Here's a fur and slips."

I smelled her perfume as she got up. Her scent eddied and whirled and followed her.

She seized the cold window bars with her hands and took a deep breath. "Just look at the stars!"

"Yes, just look at them. And if we are going to catch the gods-eye as it comes up over the horizon, we had better hurry. Here, put your things on."

We dressed quickly. I took the porto-lamp and

Beatra followed me down the dark steps, down halls, more steps, and into the great kitchen. Here I unbarred the back door. We stepped outside, and I made sure the big bronze key was safe in its hiding place behind the corner yew. Then off we went, around the great manor and up the path that led to the crest of the ridge. Goro bounded ahead as if he knew where we were going.

From the ridgetop we looked back. The great stone house lay white and silent in the starlight. The servants were doubtless still asleep, and would be for another hour yet.

The dog trotted ahead. There was no danger, of course, but it was good to have him along. Especially on account of Beatra. Years ago, when Grandfather had first begun what was now the right wing of the manor house, bears had fed in the wild berry patches in the forest edge, and wolves came down from Penn and Nyock, and perhaps from even as far north as Canda. But the place was not quite so wild, now. The forest had yielded to the plow. All around the bay rim the fields were green, and there were meadows for the cattle and horses. And beyond Grandfather's holdings there were other great houses, and cottages in their shadow, and other croplands. To go hunting now, it was necessary to journey by floater into the northern forests, and stay in our log cabin for a week or more. Ah, what fun that was. And what a relief from working in Grandfather's shops in New Bollamer. I was already planning a trip to the cabin with Beatra.

We stopped at the cliff edge. I pointed. "It should rise over the grottoes. Brother Montrey has worked out the ascension."

Beatra hunched her shoulders deeper into her furs and peered over the water. We could see nothing unusual. No moving light. We heard only the surf at the foot of the cliffs.

"Are you cold?" I asked in sudden concern.

"No. It's just the change, from the bed to here." She

moved to put me between her and the light land breeze. "What do you suppose it is, the gods-eye?"

"No one really knows. It circles the earth once a day. But we can see it only just before sunrise or just after sunset, sort of like a morning or evening star. Montrey thinks it is a great ball, hurled into the sky by the ancients. But how could they do that? And why? It doesn't make much sense."

Goro whined softly. We were all silent a moment. I searched the darkened land for a moment with narrowed eyes. "Perhaps a rabbit," I said softly. "There is still quite a bit of game out at night." I turned my head back to the horizon, then screened the lantern. "There it is."

A brilliant point of light sprang up over the distant grottoes. We watched, spellbound, hardly breathing, as it rose higher and higher.

"Ah, beautiful," whispered Beatra. The wind at her back was blowing her hair around her eyes, and she lifted a hand to brush it aside.

In that instant several shapes took silent form on our right.

By pure reflex I grabbed Beatra by the arm and started to pull her behind me. Where was Goro! Weapon? I had brought nothing. A stick... even a rock...

There was a muffled cry. A strange tongue, but I could understand the words. "Mr. President—the dog!"

And now Goro's instincts destroyed him. For twenty thousand years his ancestors had been companions to man, and had hunted with man. But always the quarry had been game—never man. Goro hesitated. For here was man, sacred man, who threatened his master, and who therefore must be killed. His hesitation was so brief it was barely detectable. But it was too much. The tall figure got off two shots. The first caught Goro in midleap, and tore his head off. Goro's corpse struck the tall one just as the gun fired again. I knew I was hit. I sank to my knees. "Beatra..." I whispered. But already the raiders were gagging her and dragging her away.

I fell over backward. I lay there, remembering those enormous owl-like eyes, those cold white cheeks, barely visible in the faintly lightening sky.

Undergrounders. I knew the myths, but until now I had not believed such people really existed.

Mr. President. That face had taken Beatra and had killed Goro. And perhaps me, Jeremy. No, not Jeremy. I was going to live.

Mr. President, we would meet again.

My eyes closed as the shining gods-eye moved slowly overhead in massive majesty.

4. Words without Sound

I FELT A strange prolonged blur, from which slow-moving images separated from time to time. It was like a long, long dream. Once or twice there was a flash of red pain, but I did not really mind, because I was outside watching it all.

Sometimes I thought I heard voices. Somehow the voices were inside me—inside my head. As though they were forming in my brain, and that my ears were quite unnecessary for this.

First voice: "He may be the man."

Second voice: "Perhaps."

First voice: "We must rely on the prophecy. We must believe that he will live, even through the test, and that he will make the journey."

Second voice: "There is the question of the darkness."

First voice: "If he is the man, all things will be provided for him."

Second voice: "Should we tell Father Phaedrus?"

First voice: "Soon. There will be time."

Second voice: "Not much time. He is dying."

Then all the voices seemed to merge together in weird and fearful harmony: "Dying...dying...dying...."

Did they mean me? I was not going to die. I refused to die. I clenched my teeth and tried to concentrate.

Now one of the images was coming out of the fuzzy background again. "Don't try to talk," said the image. The shape wore a dark gray robe, and a cowl dropped about his neck. Eyes gradually emerged from the face and peered at me.

I peered back, but my eyes were in poor focus. I closed my eyes and moved the fingers of my right hand carefully. They responded. That was good. Somehow it surprised me. I let my hand and arm move up over and beyond my chest. My fingers tried to touch the flesh of my face, but my face and head were encased in something.

The world began to howl at me. I squeezed my eyelids together as hard as I could, and brought both hands up to my head.

Things were coming back to me.

Beatra and I. And Goro, the hound. Walking up the path to the cliff edge in the dark, starlit morning. To see the god-light.

And then the figures emerging downwind out of the darkness. The shots. Beatra...? Oh, great gods! What had happened to Beatra?

I raised my hand and pointed a finger at the gray figure. I tried to talk. My lips moved, but only animal gibberish came forth.

"I told you, don't try to talk just now," admonished the gray man. "It will take time. Don't worry, you'll talk again."

I moaned.

The other was also a cowled, gray-robed figure, not quite as tall as the first. He took something from the table and showed it to me. It was a slate and a piece of chalk. "For the time being, try this."

The gray man held the slate as I slowly scraped out a word: "Beatra?"

He stood impassive a moment. "We will discuss Beatra later. First, we want you to get stronger."

It was so, then. Beatra had been taken...kidnapped. Or maybe even killed, even as Goro had been killed. I groaned. But it wasn't a proper groan. Even though it was involuntary, the sound was not quite right. Something was wrong with my voice.

I realized I was in a hospital. That much was clear. I could surmise a few things. Go back to the beginning. The servants had heard the shots. They had found me, and had taken me to the monastery surgery. That must have been several days ago. The bullet had caused brain damage, and it had affected my powers of speech.

Now *that* was curious. Was I deducing all these things, or were the men in gray talking to me? I seemed to hear their voices, and yet their lips were not moving.

There was another thing. The hazy thought was reaching me that a bit of my cerebral cortex had been snipped out, and that the surgical Friars were keeping it alive as a culture to await my disposal—if I lived.

They had done well, I thought. Why had they done well? I wasn't sure.

I scratched another word on the slate: "Grandfather?"

"Baron Wolfhead knows you are here. We will permit him to see you in a few days. Patience."

Now all this was quite extraordinary. I had been watching him carefully, and he had answered me without moving his lips. He smiled faintly.

I decided to try something. I looked at him and let a question form in my mind. "Who are you?"

"I am Brother Arcrite. I am the abbot here. And this is Brother Tien." His mouth had remained shut.

What kind of communication is this, I wondered. Words without sound? Or perhaps it really is not happening. How—

But the cowled figures had slipped away.

After they left I tried to fix them in my mind. Abbot Arcrite was a tall man, cheerful, yet grave, with an air of authority. Despite the simplicity of his garb I had the impression that he was a member of the medical team that had saved my life. His companion, Brother Tien, was (as I later learned) the chief surgeon of the monastery hospital, and had remarkable powers of healing and preservation. Because of these two good men, and others, I was alive.

Three days later I was lying quietly in bed, when I began forming the impression that Grandfather was coming to visit me. I thought I could sense the mind of the old man, taut, anxious, yet outwardly impassive, drawing nearer and nearer. Grandfather was coming up the corridor with Abbot Arcrite. There could be no mistake. The surgeon was going to permit a ten-minute visit.

Well, that was good news.

As they came into the room, I held up my hand in greeting and grinned at my grandfather. The old man strode over to the bedside and took my hand. "Yes, Jeremy, yes, yes, it is I. They would not let me see you until now..." He took a kerchief from his jacket pocket, wiped his eyes, then blew his nose with authority. "They think now you will live. They say I can spend a few minutes with you."

"Ten minutes," warned Abbot Arcrite. "That's all. When I come back, Baron Wolfhead, you will have to leave." He closed the door behind him.

I looked at Grandfather's face in wonder and love.

The old man cleared his throat. "I am told you have a little speech problem. So I will have to do the talking. You must listen. Which is only right and proper, because after all I am your grandfather, and my gray hairs should command a little respect."

I nodded.

"So I guess you want to know everything? What

happened, and all events since that night?"

I nodded again.

"Well, Jeremy, it isn't so good." He peered at me earnestly. "But I think you are able to know the worst?"

I looked at him expectantly. I seemed to see the hesitant shadows forming in the old man's mind. I knew what was coming. I knew exactly what he was going to say.

"Ansel and Sligh heard the shots from the direction of the cliff. They scrambled about for their clothes and for their guns, which they finally found, after much useless squealing and wasted motion, for the weapons were over the mantel in the trophy room, where they have always been kept. And being duly clothed and armed, they ran, with great fear and trembling, out toward the cliff rim, and there they found you and Goro. But no Beatra. Beatra was gone. And they carried you back, holding you between them. There was a great deal of blood, and they thought you were dead. But then one of them found a heartbeat, so they got you into the floater, and brought you here to the abbey medicos. Ansel made many mistakes, and got lost several times, but finally he got you here. He has not much skill in driving the floater. But he made great efforts, and you owe your life to him and Sligh."

I picked up the slate and wrote in fair uncial script: "Thank them."

"Yes. Of course. I already have."

I wrote again. "What will happen to Beatra?"

The old man hesitated. "I think she lives." His face was hard, stone carved. "The elders have met on this, Jeremy. We put the question to the computer. There are several possibilities, alternate explanations. Perhaps you could help us narrow the possibilities. Did you see any of their faces?"

I wrote: "Very pale. Undergrounders, I think."

"Yes, undergrounders. We found skid marks of a floater. They probably came from a tunnel exit a few miles away. Possibly from one of the sea caves."

"Why topside?"

"Like you and Beatra. To see the gods-eye."

"Why take Beatra?"

"The alternate was to kill her. According to the stories, the undergrounders periodically send up raiding parties to take captives for questioning. And sometimes women."

I flinched.

He continued. "Our information on such activities goes back some twenty-odd years when...a captive...escaped. Or was perhaps released, and told the Friars all he could about life underground. The undergrounders are said to keep up to date on our progress in this way."

I knew the tale. According to the Returner, the entire Federal Government in Washton had gone underground three thousand years ago, just before the Desolation, and the present undergrounders were their descendants. They had named their underground city, Dis, for the vanished District of Columbia. (This name, Dis, some said, had nothing to do with the District of Columbia, but was actually the Hell City of Dis in the great Prophet Dante's *Inferno*.) Once I had thought it all an amusing myth. Well, now I knew it was no fairy tale. I had met their President.

I wrote: "Beatra—alive?"

"There is good reason to think so."

"Rescue?"

"You mean gather a soldier band and go after her?" The old man turned his head away. "Not as easy as you think, Jeremy. I offered twenty gold pieces for each man, trained or untrained. Four volunteered. This was out of the entire shire of New Bollamer. And understand, even if I had offered fifty thousand, it would not be enough. We cannot overcome them underground, just as they cannot overcome us aboveground. We live in different worlds. We cannot

fight in darkness, and they cannot fight in daylight.
There is no good way to grapple with them. One man
alone would probably do about as well as an army.
Except that he might be killed a little quicker. I thought
of going myself. But it wasn't realistic. They would
simply kill me. And what good would I be to you, if I
were dead? No, Jeremy, remember Beatra, but
remembering, you must learn to forget. When you are
able to walk about, we will talk to her people, and
arrange her funeral. We will consult the stonecutters,
and we will design a magnificent cenotaph, in black
granite, well polished. We'll leave room for an
inscription, if you care to add one."

I thought to myself, write this for her: She lives!

But now I sensed Abbot Arcrite returning up the
corridor. Was there anything I had to tell Grandfather?
One thing, perhaps. I wrote on the slate: "Bury Goro."

"I did. With honors. He tried."

I nodded. And yet I wondered. With honors? Goro
had hesitated. For that split second, Goro had
hesitated. Not because he had been afraid, but because
he was a dog called upon to attack a man. What would
be, then, the ideal guardian animal? It would have to
attack my enemies instantly, human or nonhuman.
Only a wild creature would do this.

And now Brother Arcrite came in. He and
Grandfather bowed to each other.

"Time is up," said the abbot.

After they left I lay there thinking. I thought of
Beatra, and a great ache grew in my vitals. To relieve
the pain, I attempted to double up. But it was no use. I
thought of Beatra, at table, taking me to work in the
floater, sitting with me on the marble benches in front
of the fountain in the statuary garden. I saw the glint of
fire in her eyes, I heard her laughter like little bells, and
the pain became so great that I tried to scream. The
effort brought me peace, because I fainted.

A week later I was permitted to take short walks in the garden, and it was here that Abbot Arcrite brought a certain man to meet me.

This was a very curious encounter.

Although I had sensed that Brother Tien and another were about to come around the hedge, I was totally unprepared for what I saw.

Tien's companion was an old man, a shattered husk. He glided into view seated in a chairfloater. It stopped at my bench, with Brother Tien close behind. I knew chairfloaters existed, but I had never before seen one. The aged and infirm used them on occasion. And sometimes the very rich, out of vanity rather than true need. I could see that, with this man, it was a case of necessity. For he seemed very old indeed. His gray woolen robe covered all of him except his face and hands, which were brown and shriveled, and (it seemed to me then) declared him at least a centenarian. His eyes were closed. His arms and legs, shrunken as twigs in winter, were motionless. His head was supported by a foam plastic collar. Indeed, the only movement to his whole body was the barely perceptible rhythmic rise and fall of his chest.

"Father Phaedrus," said Tien, "Jeremy Wolfhead."

I arose and bowed. And stared.

Father Phaedrus' thought came to me, almost as clearly as if he had spoken. "Yes, my son, I am completely paralyzed."

I blurted mentally, "Then how do you manage the chairfloater?"

"The controls respond to my mental command. Brother Tien did everything. He designed the hover-chair. He headed the surgical team that blended me and this chair into a unitary machine. I am Brother Tien's handiwork." He seemed to study me curiously, hungrily, though his eyelids opened not a fraction of an inch. His mind shield was closed tightly, but not enough to hide a seething and frothing behind it.

Abbot Arcrite broke the tension by clearing his throat ostentatiously. "Jeremy, my son," he began, "I have somewhat to say to you. I will start with a bit of history."

Father Phaedrus moved his hoverchair opposite my bench and set it down silently on the turf.

"As you know," continued the abbot, "during the Desolation, and after, a number of mutations developed in many of the residual life forms. Human beings were no exception. Most of these mutations were bad, and resulted in extinction of the new species. A very few were beneficial, and contributed to survival. One such is what the geneticists call the telepathic mutation. The power of speech may be temporarily lost, but the subject can now read minds, and can plant his own thoughts in the minds of others. It all takes place because of changes in the parietal lobe of the cerebrum. Sometimes the mutation lies latent. It can be activated overnight, by causes unknown. Or it can be activated by a blow to the parietal area. In your case, it was activated by a blow that broke the skull cap."

The abbot walked over to the little garden table, and we placed ourselves around it. Father Phaedrus moved his chair to join us.

"The telepathic mutation," continued the abbot, "sometimes—not always—brings with it other possibilities. Now, Brother Tien . . ."

The surgeon picked a dry blade of grass from the lawn, broke off a tiny piece, and dropped it on the white marble table top.

"Proceed," said Abbot Arcrite mentally.

Tien stared at the little piece of grass. It jumped upward, then hovered an inch over the table surface. "It is 'psi-movement,'" explained the abbot. "The ancients first named it. There were genetic traces of the trait even in their day."

During all this Father Phaedrus sat immobile and mute in his hoverchair at Arcrite's side. But I knew he was completely absorbed in the proceedings, and especially in my reaction.

Aside from his nearly total physical disability I noted a further disconcerting aspect of Father Phaedrus. He was intrusive. He continually, eagerly, sought access to the innermost reaches of my mind. Out of respect for his condition, and in view of the obvious difference in our ages, I did not admonish him for this. I simply clamped down my mind shield as best I could. And finally he retreated, but unabashed.

I addressed a mental question to Brother Tien. "What is the maximum weight you can lift?"

The Friar's thought came back to me immediately. "About five pounds, but it has to be balanced, to provide a vortex."

"Explain that."

Tien walked over to the pathway and picked up a handful of tiny pebbles. He put them on the table. Two by two they left the table surface and began spinning in the air about a common center.

I was fascinated. My eyes shifted back and forth from his face, now beginning to sweat, and then to the pebble vortex, which was now a foot off the table, and spinning with a loud whine.

I wondered whether I dared ask Brother Tien a question while the vortex was in motion. He answered me mentally, before I even framed the words in my mind. "Yes. It can move laterally." The spinning mass moved slowly away from the table and hovered in the air over a bed of lilies.

"It could be dangerous," I mused.

"Very. Watch that toadstool."

The vortex moved over a large white amanita, paused a moment, then plunged toward it. There was a brief flurry of moist flying particles, and a sound like a circular saw chewing into a knot of wood.

And then the dust settled, and I saw a declivity in the ground where the turf had been dug away, a full inch deep and six inches in diameter.

I stared, first at the hole, then at Brother Tien.

Abbot Arcrite said to me (and I detected grim overtones in his statement): "You are wondering if you can do that. We don't know. In any case, the power comes in stages, and there is much training involved."

I had a sudden vision. There was that harsh albino face, and here came this pebbly whirlwind, churning into it. Ah...

"If you wish," said Arcrite, "we can give you a preliminary test."

"Now!" I formed the word in my mind.

"Yes," said Abbot Arcrite. His tone seemed grave.

"Yes," said Father Phaedrus. He seemed downright grim.

Why the lack of enthusiasm, I wondered. Wasn't this their idea, in the first place?

"You will see, and understand," said the abbot cryptically.

And that was all I could get from them.

5. THE STRESS TEST

"WE CAN START here and now," said Abbot Arcrite. Brother Tien plucked a grass tip from the sward at his feet and dropped it to the table top. "Concentrate," said the abbot. "Try to lift it from the table."

I leaned forward. I concentrated. I willed that it lift. I commanded it. But the bit of green did not move. Again I tried. My brows corrugated, and I broke out in a sweat. For Beatra's sake, I thought, you will rise.

But the stupid thing simply lay there.

Arcrite touched minds briefly with Tien and Father Phaedrus.

I sensed words forming in the abbot's mind. "It is not necessarily determinative. He is not under stress."

"Stress?" I asked mentally.

Tien and Arcrite looked away.

Finally Father Phaedrus said: "There is a definitive test for vortectic power. You could undertake the stress determination." A shimmering gray-red danger signal overlay his thought.

"I gather," I said in my mind, "that if I have this

talent, it will certainly come forth during what you call the stress test?"

"Yes," agreed Abbot Arcrite. (Did he hesitate?)

"And if I don't have it?"

And now they were all deliberately shielding their thoughts from me. Curtains went up. I caught only glimpses of things. Of a cell-like room. Of something deadly whizzing toward me. Of a shield. Crunch. But *what* had crunched? What would happen to me? Suddenly I did not like any of it.

The abbot looked at Father Phaedrus for a moment. I caught traces of a mental exchange. The paralytic was adamant. The abbot turned back to me. "We can show you," he said finally. "You can then choose for yourself. We can take you through it, step by step. You will be free to stop it at any time."

"*Almost* any time," corrected Brother Tien.

Father Phaedrus said nothing. I knew he was "watching" me intently.

"I would like to try it," I said. "When do I start?"

"Now, if you like," said the abbot. "We need only walk across the square to the studio."

And so we did.

The studio was a smallish room, but well lit. At one end was an iron scaffolding. We went over to it. It was then that I noticed the straps on the iron bars. And the dark red stains at the foot of the structure.

They were bloodstains, and they cried out to me. A man had recently died here. And others before him. What had led the owners of this precious fluid to risk it so readily? Readily? Perhaps they, like myself, had second thoughts at the end. Perhaps in those last milliseconds, when they saw the crashing face of disaster, they cried out, No! No! But too late. Ready or not, they died. For this seems to be the nature of death. We risk it. We seek it out. We welcome brushes with it. We court it. But when it turns to embrace us, we cry out, "Not yet!"

I tried hard to swallow, but found I could not.

Now this showed a sudden sinister side to the Brothers that I had never before suspected. I suddenly realized that all of them had to pass this test before they were admitted to the Brotherhood. And that not all candidates were successful.

"I do not wish to become a Brother," I said bluntly. "I have other plans. With all respect," I added hastily.

"You need not become one of us," said Abbot Arcrite. "And we respect your own personal plans. You know that men have died in taking the stress test. You have wondered why they would risk their lives for so paltry a treasure as the vortectic talent. We can now tell you a little. Our prime directive was stated for us three thousand years ago: destroy the gods-eye. How? Through the powers of the vortex. And this means that through the centuries we have maintained a pool of vortectic talent."

Were they all mad? "But *why*?" I demanded. "Why ask men to risk death for so futile a goal? Even if you were able, why would you want to destroy that perfectly harmless orbiting light speck?"

"If we do not, we fear that it will eventually kill you, and us, and every living creature on the face of the earth," said the abbot simply.

This was too much. "And how do you propose to destroy it?" I asked.

"It is controlled from underground," said the abbot. "Someone will have to go there."

Aha! Their interest in me suddenly began to make sense. But I wanted no part of their game. The gods-eye wasn't bothering me. It had been inert for as long as men could remember and it wasn't likely to change.

Father Phaedrus spoke to me. "Jeremy, my son," he said bluntly, "I think you must try the test, even though you fail, and die."

There it was, laid out in the open. I felt unable to argue with him.

"Well," I said, "at least I can start."

The abbot shrugged his shoulders. "Strapping in is the first step. You can still discontinue after that—up to a point."

My heart was pounding. "Strap me in."

Tien buckled the straps around my arms, legs, and waist. I could not move a fraction of an inch in any direction. "There is a shield, isn't there?" I demanded.

"You read well, Jeremy," said the abbot. "Yes, there is a shield." Already Brother Tien was wheeling up a big metal plate. He positioned it in front of me, so that it covered, or seemed to cover, all of my body except my eyes.

"The protection is illusory," said the abbot dryly. "There is a tiny hole in the plate directly in front of your heart. Lights off, please."

My heart began to throb even faster. Something, a deadly missile of some kind, was aimed straight at my heart. What kind of test was this?

Father Phaedrus broke into my thoughts. "Jeremy," he stated brusquely, "do not be afraid. You *must* do this, and you *can* do it!"

I smiled crookedly. Nothing was aimed at *his* heart.

"You are wrong, Jeremy," he said.

The room was plunged into semidarkness. A pencil of light stabbed toward me from the opposite end of the room. "Quite harmless," said the abbot. "Simply for purposes of alignment. The light beam must go through the hole."

"Ah," I thought.

"No, you do not yet understand," chided the abbot.

"What, then?"

"Next," said Tien, "we release the dust curtain."

Two yards in front of me a coin-sized disk of bright light appeared to intersect the little light beam. And then I realized that a thin curtain of dust was falling from a container in the ceiling down to a gutter in the floor. The light pencil was simply reflecting from the dust particles at the plane of intersection. The disk was the reflected intersection. And now I had it—or most of it. "A precision cross-bow fires a thin metal arrow through the dust," I said. "If nothing is done, it passes through the hole in the shield and enters my heart."

"True," said the abbot.

"How do I make it not pass through the hole in the shield?"

"If you have the talent," said the abbot, "your subconscious mind will take over and act by reflex. It will instantly develop a dust vortex where the arrow must pass through the light disk. The vortex will deflect the arrow very slightly, enough to make it miss the hole in the shield. It will then break harmlessly against the shield."

"And if I don't deflect the arrow?"

"Your question is of course superfluous."

"Who releases the arrow?" I asked.

"You do."

Raw, I thought to myself. Quite raw. By my own hand. "Suppose I am successful," I said to them. "Suppose I find I have the talent. Will I have to wait for another life and death situation before I can use it again?"

"No, once established, you will be able to call it forth at will."

It was something to ponder. Yet I think I had already made up my mind. Perhaps I did not tell them instantly for the simple reason that I wanted another thirty seconds of life. Yes, life was sweet, and if I were about to take leave of it, I wanted my reasons laid out in good array.

Their motives, their reasons, were not the same as mine. These three were playing a deeper game. To them, and for their own private reasons, something involving the gods-eye, it was apparently essential that I go underground, and to do this and survive there, I had to pass their tests. But I was totally unmoved by their reasons. I had to have my own.

I was going after Beatra. I knew that, and they knew it. And we all knew I couldn't take any kind of weapon. Nothing of wood or metal. Nothing of any artificial structure. We knew, from the reports of the Returner, that the undergrounders had detectors in their sea cave entrance that would detect such things and sound an immediate alarm. I would be found and killed within the hour of my attempted entry. No weapons. I would have to enter that dismal place stripped absolutely naked. I would need this talent—if in fact I had it. It was my only chance. For it would be a living weapon, a thing I could carry with me, in my mind, on call at all times.

I had to know. Father Phaedrus knew me well—I had to try, even though I died.

If I did not have the talent then Beatra would die, or perhaps worse would be done to her. But I would be dead, and know nothing of it. (Unless what the godcallers say is true, that we would meet again in some other kind of existence, after death. But what that could be, I have no idea.) If I failed with the arrow, death would be quick and almost painless. Not that I am afraid of pain. I have been hurt before, in hunting trips. I have been clawed, and I have had some broken bones. But it had been done to me by hunted things, and perhaps I had no excuse or complaint. Well, now I was the hunted thing, the cornered quarry.

I gave the mental command: "Hand me the release button." Abbot Arcrite handed me a fist-sized thing with the little plunger sticking out. There was no cord. It worked by radio.

I did not think anymore.

I peered fixedly at that wavering disk of light in the dust curtain, and I pushed the plunger firmly with my thumb.

Time stood still—almost. The dust curtain seemed fixed in space. It was not falling anymore. At least, I could not see any movement. And then a tiny stem of metal slowly pierced the lighted circle of the dust curtain. I studied it with a certain detached curiosity. It kept coming. Now some three inches had passed through the curtain. How long is it going to be, I wondered. It will be all day before it reaches me. Nothing to worry about, really.

And now I could see the end of it emerging. I saw the beginning tips of the three stablizer vanes on its tail.

It was going to get through, and I had done nothing!

I now experienced a strange sensory rhapsody. I saw Beatra. She was dancing on the stone flags of our bedroom. I could hear the soft swish of her sandals on the hard polished surface. She was singing, and I heard her. It was springtime, and a soft breeze was blowing through the curtains in the bay window. I smelled the tantalizing odor of wild cherry pollen. Did this mean that I was about to die? But if I died, who would rescue her? It must not be! Mentally I shrieked, "Beatra!"

My mind began churning. I tried to cry out, but nothing came out of my throat. But something within my mind *fixed* on the dust on the right-hand side of the vanes. The dust there began to whirl. I could see the little eddy. It was spinning, faster and faster. It made the fletches wobble. The head of the arrow was kicked out of its straight-line path. And here it came. Time was speeding up.

Ping!

I knew where it had hit. A good five inches to the left of the hole in the shield. And then it had rebounded.

I collapsed. I hung there in my straps, gurgling.

But I had it. I knew I had it.

I was ecstatic but exhausted. But perhaps not totally exhausted. They had promised me that I could call up my new gift at will.

My eyes were closed. I left them that way. I knew the dust curtain had stopped falling. I knew there was an accumulation of dust on the studio floor. As I hung there slack in the straps, I began to gather up that dust, a pinch at a time, balancing each grain by another grain, one after another, and I began to make them whirl. Faster and faster. The Brothers watched impassively. I knew what the particles were made of. A type of feldspar. Very hard, very abrasive.

I lifted the vortex. I made it move toward me, a thing alive. I changed its shape at will. It was a sphere. It was a cylinder. As it came up to my metal shield, I transformed it into a disk, whining, lethal. I could make it do anything I wanted. I could make it cut the straps that held me. I could make it cut the iron bars of the scaffold.

I sensed alarm in the minds of Abbot Arcrite and Brother Tien. But Father Phaedrus seemed to be laughing.

But I would not be that destructive.

Their minds relaxed.

However: I dropped the arrow-starter from my right hand. Before it had fallen to my waist, the whirling disk had sliced it in half.

The abbot released me. Enough for one day.

I thought I caught a flash of strange mental interplay between Phaedrus and the abbot.

Phaedrus: "I think he is the one."

Arcrite: "He may be indeed."

Phaedrus: "My time to prophesy is drawing very close. We will soon know."

"Nay, good father, you have years to go."

I understood nothing of this.

And now Phaedrus seemed suddenly to collapse in his hoverchair, which sat down hard on the stone flooring. His companions rushed over in alarm. From his flickering mind, I caught a garbled mental message: "I'll steal that floater...down the river...I'll get away from them yet...where does the river lead...I'm falling...! Ahhh...!"

Poor Phaedrus. The strain of rising from his sick

bed had been too much for him. I suspected that this was not a unique occurrence—that he probably alternated between periods of clarity and incoherence, that initially I had seen his best side for an hour, and now he was exposing a darker side.

His mind had collapsed; probably it had been awry for years.

But the scene was not prolonged. Abbot Arcrite was already wheeling him out of the building. I did not see Father Phaedrus again for several weeks.

As the days passed, my vortex training continued.

"We used dust initially because you could see it and feel it," said Abbot Arcrite. "Also because the telekinetic effect increases in proportion to the number of particles, and in inverse proportion to their size. And yet, there are much smaller and much more numerous particles available. They surround us, in fact. I mean ambient air. We can do a number of things with these tiny molecules. In the first place, suppose you need a light source. Well now, what is light? It is photons, a radiant form of energy produced when an electron slips outward from one orbit to another." He drew the blind and turned off the light. "Permit me to demonstrate." I sat there quietly, and in a matter of seconds a pale blue sphere formed in the air in front and above the abbot. A soft glow flickered over the room, then faded as the globe disappeared. "Try it," said the abbot.

I concentrated. I saw, as though through some great microscope, countless tiny dumbbells swimming in front of my eyes. Without thinking about it, I knew they were individual oxygen and nitrogen molecules. I moved in deeper. I concentrated on one single molecule. I sensed eight tiny charged particles stationed in mysterious shells about a comparatively massive central nucleus. Oxygen. I poured energy into one of the tiny particles in the outermost shell, and it shifted into a shell even farther away from the nucleus, and simultaneously it released a sparklet. One photon. And now I was doing the same thing to dozens of other molecules. Hundreds. Oxygen and nitrogen. Millions. They had no number. They whirled, and a luminous sphere filled the room with light, so much light that I had to close my eyes, and the abbot held his hands over his face. "It is enough," he said.

Day after day the training continued. I learned how to make a small whirlwind that could suck things into its spinning recesses and carry them from one end of the room to the other. They taught me how a vortex can be a heat pump, heat being drained away from the center and released at the periphery. In another experiment I froze a glass of water in thirty seconds. Using the same technique, I connected two lengths of copper wire to a small electric motor. One length I heated with the outside of a spinning sphere of air and the other length I cooled with the inside of a second spinning air sphere. The system actually developed a small electric current, and the electric motor hummed merrily. The Brothers looked at it, then at each other, in wondering approval. They had never seen an engineering application of the vortex. I wished that Grandfather had been there to see it. But perhaps it was just as well that he wasn't there. He would not have believed it anyway!

6. BEATRA'S FUNERAL

WE MADE THE arrangements with Godcaller Hander. I had wanted a simple ceremony, something suitable for her kinsmen and mine, held at the village kirk. But her father and brothers would have none of it. They wanted a great thing starting on the square, with all the villagers, and then moving to their family dead-acre. It was not a thing to quarrel about, so I gave in.

I had already seen the headstone. Grandfather had ordered it from the stonecutter—polished black granite. The legend read:

> Beatra Wolfhead
> Born 1880
> Died 1900

Like most legends, it mingled truth and fiction.

Grandfather also provided the coffin. It was a heavy, ornate thing, trimmed in silver and ivory, and I think he had been saving it for himself. It seemed illogical to bury it empty. But that was the way the thing went. So far as her family was concerned, she was dead, and it was my fault. If she wasn't in that box, she might as well be.

They carried the coffin from Grandfather's warehouse by truckfloater. And when Godcaller Hander saw how heavy it was, he knew right away that no number of shoulders, no matter how strong and willing, could march away with it to the dead-acre. So they left it on the floater and simply laid a purple satin drape over it.

Hander started things by invoking a blessing on her immortality, and then asked God to forgive me for letting her be taken away. During all this Beatra's father did not bow his head in grief and humility. Instead he glared at me. Well, perhaps he was justified. I hung my bandaged head. I should have expected the danger, and I should never have exposed her to it. At the very least, I should have carried a weapon. And so it had come to this.

The Godcaller now lined up the forty mourners, got them in reasonable tune, and off we went, down the hill, through the village, and off through the countryside. Beatra's family followed the coffinfloater, Grandfather and I were next, and then the ragtag collection of villagers, who would not miss any of it for the world.

It was the longest three miles I have ever journeyed. The sun was bright; there was a slight breeze, and it shook loose a fog of pollen from the wild cherry trees that lined the road. I will never forget the scent of those trees. It took me back to the night of the winter ball.

At the gravesite we regrouped. Grandfather and I took one side of the open pit, Beatra's family the other. The Godcaller stood at one end with his psalter, and the gravedigger at the other with his shovel. It was all quite insane and a waste of time and emotion, for Beatra was alive. I knew this. She was certainly not in that heavy teakwood box, and none of this could have the slightest effect on her. This was for her family. I suppose they had a right to have this (they thought) final chapter of her lifebook read to them.

While the Godcaller read his psalm, Grandfather and I on one side, and her father and brother on the other, lowered the coffin into the grave with the heavy hempen ropes. Then we pulled the ropes back out and tossed them to the gravedigger. He thrust his shovel into the waiting pile of dirt and tossed a shovelful on the waiting box. There was a faint hollow ring. Then again, and again. Then he waited while Beatra's father pulled his dagger from its sheath and walked around to my side of the grave.

I pulled off my tunic, baring myself to the waist.

He looked at me grimly, without sorrow or forgiveness, then made the first cut of the cross upon my chest. The blood spurted. I did not move a muscle. "Carry her memory thus," he intoned. Then he made the second cut to complete the cross. More blood. Quite a bit more than was necessary, but I was not inclined to complain. "She dies barren," he said, "as barren as that box." He wiped the blade on his breeches, then walked away.

In that moment I regained my voice. I found myself whispering, "No! She lives!"

7. THE ABBOT ADVISES

THE DAY AFTER the funeral, Brother Tien removed my head bandages. The abbot made it a point to be present. He sent a thought to me. "We know that you are determined to seek your wife underground. We have certainly encouraged you. Nevertheless, we ask you to consider—are you doing this as a socially acceptable means of suicide, or will you plan your journey with the greatest possible skill and with a thorough understanding of the obstacles to be overcome?"

That was too complicated for me. "I'm going down, and I will bring Beatra out or die." I looked across the room at the polished metal mirror. The cut of my hair was pretty crude, and I could see and feel a bristly stubble over my forehead, where they had evidently shaved my skull before sawing it open. There was a slight declivity there. That was where they had chopped out a bit of my cerebral cortex, inserted a protective metal plate, and pulled the skin back over it. But otherwise I could detect no damage. Physically, thanks to the Brothers, I had pulled through beautifully. I suddenly remembered my manners. "Abbot Arcrite, I would welcome any help or advice you can give me."

"You answer well. Let me consider then. To avoid instant detection, you will have to look like the undergrounders. Your skin is tanned. You will have to lighten it to a pale white. Brother Tien will provide the necessary bleaching oils. Start using them daily, after your morning shower." He studied my yellow hair and blue eyes. "Satisfactory, although the eyes may be somewhat small by underground standards. But there's no help for it." He paused. "And now we have a serious problem, yet not one beyond solution. It will be dark underground. The people there have adjusted to the darkness over the three thousand years since the Desolation. Their pupils are much larger than ours. But the dim lighting can offer serious problems for one of us. Brother Tien will explain this to you."

"Yes," said Tien mentally. "According to the Returner, they have three levels of lighting, or lack of it. First they have, what are to them, 'high-intensity' lights. These are ceiling lights in their administrative buildings, many of their homes, street corners, search beams on their floaters, and so on. The degree of illumination is roughly equivalent to twilight or dusk here.

"Second, most of the street ceilings, as well as many houses and rooms, are coated with a fluorescent pigment. It receives invisible radiation energy from some very mysterious unknown source, penetrating through yards, aye, perhaps even miles of rock strata and walls, and the pigment converts this energy into visible radiation. After an initial adjustment, you should be able to make out the shapes of gross objects, such as vehicles, furniture, people, and so on. But you will not be able to distinguish faces nor to read print. You may find it somewhat like starlight on a clear, moonless night. To the undergrounders, however, this gives ample light to conduct their daily affairs. By this light, they can drive their vehicles, read books, till their fields, and aim a gun at you. You would not be able to do any of this, except that you *might* be able to manage a floater in light traffic."

I was puzzled. "But why not simply make a light-ball? That would take care of any degree of darkness."

Brother Tien laughed shortly. "And announce your presence for miles around?" He continued. "Finally, there is total darkness. There is no wall pigment or other light source available. This is the general case in the outlying grottoes and caverns, and the corridors that link them into the city. There is only one known species of life capable of 'seeing' in such darkness. This is the dire wolf, a mutant that has evolved only since the Desolation. It can 'see' to some extent by means of thermal differentiation in the infrared."

I looked at him in wonder. A dire wolf? Next to the great white bear, the deadliest creature in North America. To penetrate into the semilighted areas of the underground city, I needed a dire wolf. Not just any dire wolf. This one would have to be as obedient as a dog, and capable of telepathic communication.

They had followed my thoughts. "Yes, telepathic communication," said the abbot. "Why do you think we saved that bit of your cranial tissue?"

"The perfect implant for a wolf brain," confirmed Tien.

I was amazed. And puzzled.

"Would I 'talk' mentally to the wolf the same way I'm communicating with you two now?"

"Very much the same," said Brother Tien. "The difference would be that your thoughts, as well as those of the animal, would be coded through the transplant. For example, suppose you want to say to the wolf, 'Kill.' Your own brain breaks down the command into its components of alpha, beta, and gamma waves.

These are sent to the transplant, which reconstitutes them into messages to the appropriate areas of the lupine cortex, where they are translated into wolf language. When the animal talks to you, the process is simply reversed."

"Nothing to it, really," said the abbot firmly.

"All you need is a wolf," said Brother Tien.

I was already making plans.

8. THE WOLF

THAT VERY AFTERNOON I took the floater and made north to the Delara Valley. I had heard rumors that a trapper had captured, perhaps a year ago, a pair of dire wolf cubs, one male, one female, and was raising them as though they were dogs. The report was that he lived alone and hated human company, but seemed to need companionship, especially during the long winters.

Perhaps I should explain about those winters. Our scientists tell us that after the Desolation it became very cold all over the world, because of the great palls of dust which for years and years blotted out the sun. In those days it snowed winter and summer, and the snows did not melt, but piled into great thick sheets of ice all over the land. And then the ice began to *flow*, but slowly, like cold honey. And it flowed into the river valleys, pushing rocks and dirt and mud ahead of it. All of that happened a long time ago, and the ice is gone now, at least in the New Bollamer area. Nevertheless I have hunted in the Delara Valley, and I can tell you that there is still ice there, even in summer. There is a long mass of ice in the middle of the valley, a thousand yards thick. A river runs under it, into a long lake shaped like a finger. Grandfather, who has never been this far north, says that the ice melts more and more each year, and that the ice face retreats up the valley more and more, and that someday it will be melted altogether. Well, of course, Grandfather is a scientist, and he can say what he wants, and there will be no one who will disagree with him, at least to his face. Certainly not I. But one thing is sure—in winter, that valley must be the coldest place on our northern seaboard. And snow? I have hunted there at times when I have had to shoe-shoe over snow ten yards thick, and more falling. And if you are shut up in a cabin on Lake Delara over the winter, you might be glad for the companionship of even a dire wolf. So I can understand that trapper.

I dropped the floater in a clearing by the skinning house and hit the horn with my thumb. The cacophonous blast echoed horridly back and forth between the valley walls.

The cabin door opened a few inches. A gruff voice called out: "Stop that racket or I'll blow your head off!" And indeed, a rifle barrel moved forward out of the door crack, pointed with some accuracy at my head. "State your business!" he shouted.

"I'd like to buy something," I called out.

"Buy something? Well, now..."

Trapper Thornhouse stepped out on the rickety porch. He was followed by two of the handsomest wolves I have ever seen. One was gray, about twenty-seven inches at the shoulder. Probably the male. The other was white and somewhat smaller. The female. At that instant I found a name for her. For, even as the poet Virgil had guided Dante to the City of Dis in the great prophecy, so would the wolf Virgil guide me in my journey down to Dis. I knew immediately that I would leave here with her.

And now I could read the trapper's thoughts clearly. A patchwork of mingled suspicion, curiosity, and greed. He reasoned that I needed something badly and was willing to pay. How much could he get from me?

There was going to be trouble. I had already attached my narco-dart gun to my thumbnail, but I had wanted to save the dart for Virgil. I'd have to sedate her to get her into the porto-cage. I didn't want to waste the dart on this idiot. But there were other ways to handle Thornhouse. I noted the small stones, leaves, dirt, and debris scattered about the clearing. I wasn't worried.

I stepped slowly and carefully out of the floater and on to the ground.

The wolves began to growl. The sounds came from deep within their throats, and it was a fearsome thing.

"Quiet, friends," said the trapper. "Let's see what he has to say. And then... we'll see."

I pointed at Virgil. "I'd like to buy her. How much?"

He rubbed his chin and studied me, the floater, and then looked down at Virgil. The wolves stayed with him and stood at his knee, still as statues. I couldn't keep my eyes off her. How beautiful she was!

I already knew what he was going to say. "Can't sell her, sonny. She's part of my little family. So I guess I can't help you, and I guess you had better skedaddle." (He knew I wasn't about to leave.)

I pulled a leather bag from my pocket. I dangled it against my other palm. He heard the clink of metal. I loosened the drawstring and took out a handful of gold pieces. "All this for the female," I said. His eyes widened. "How about it?" I said.

He rubbed his chin again. Contact with the grease, grime, and soup drippings in that unlovely felted mass seemed to increase his brainpower. He shook his head. "Is *that* all?" he demanded. "Just gold? I can't spend gold here. Not a trading village within twenty miles."

With an eye on his rifle barrel, I backed carefully to

the cockpit of the floater and brought out a steel bow and case of fitted arrows. I handed them to him. He hefted the bow appreciatively.

"Stainless metal," I said. "Worth a lot of money. Good pull. Silent arrows. You can make a second kill."

"What else?"

"That's all I have."

A low and cunning thought was forming in his mean little skull. "Throw in the floater, and you can have her."

"Don't be stupid, trapper. How would I get the wolf out?"

He brought his rifle up again. I estimated that the bullet would enter about midway between my eyes. Grandfather would never find my body here. First my parents, then Beatra, then me. It would be too much for him.

But perhaps it wouldn't come to that.

Thornhouse was still ruminating, and I read him clearly. He was trying to make up his mind whether to tell me to leave everything and walk out of his valley, or whether he should kill me. What he really wanted was the floater. If he had a floater he could trap all the way up into Canda. Candian pelts brought twice as much money as local skins. Also, it would simplify things all around to kill me. That way I couldn't return with friends breathing vengeance. Meanwhile he would hide the floater back in the glen, and if anyone came looking for me, he would claim ignorance.

So he would kill me. Now. Safely. Without complications.

His finger tightened on his trigger. But he was not nearly fast enough.

Time slowed for me again. I summoned up a whirlpool of pebbles, dirt, dust, leaves, whatever there was within a radius of several yards around the trio. They were blinded. My would-be executioner screamed, dropped his rifle, and tried to cover his eyes with his hands. One of the animals bolted out of the whirlstream and fled in a gray streak toward the cabin. And a flash of white burst out of the storm, aimed straight at my throat. I didn't have time to be elated at her readiness to attack. I fired my dart at her in midair, and she dropped at my feet.

I let the dust settle around the feet of the trapper. He was a comic sight. His clothing hung about him in shreds. He was now nearly bald, and almost clean shaven. A single tuft of hair stuck up from the top of his head, and it was twisted into a tight spiral.

I laughed at him.

Virgil had collapsed and was in the act of rolling on her side. The dart was still stuck in her chest. It had done its work well, but she would be paralyzed for only a couple of minutes.

I picked up the trapper's rifle, broke out the electros, and dropped the weapon at his feet. I put the bag of gold back in my pocket, retrieved the bow and arrow, and put them all back in the floater pit. Next I got out the folding pen, set it up quite casually, and then went over and picked up my new friend. Ah, how rich and thick was her fur! Even in her dazed condition she managed a throaty growl. I smiled.

I got her stowed away, climbed into the floater without a backward glance at my dazed host, and headed south.

9. A TRANSPLANT

"THE WOLF BRAIN is basically the same as any other mammalian brain—including yours," said Brother Tien. "Certain features are of course accentuated, while others are repressed. Areas dealing with scent, hearing, and sight are enlarged, as might be expected. Words and sentences, which you have in neighboring areas of the temporal, parietal, and frontal lobes, have no counterpart areas in the brain of the dire wolf. Also, in the wolf there is little provision for mental process in depth. The frontal lobe, for example, is minuscule."

Virgil was stretched out on her belly on the operating table. Her head was strapped, chin down, against a wooden block support. She was covered with a white drape. There was a square hole in the drape over the top of her skull, which had been shaved.

They had encased me in sterile gown and mask, and they were letting me watch the operation.

"We have never done it before," said Tien. "However, it is fairly simple, both in theory and in technique. It ought to work."

The nurse handed him a scalpel and he sliced a capital "H" on the animal's forehead. Then he pulled back the two skin flaps and fastened them. I winced.

He got to work with an audio drill and cut through the bone. The nurse handed him a sponge. He daubed at the blood and threw the sponge on the floor.

Now he folded back a flap of bone. He motioned for me to take a look. "That is the dura mater—a protective sheath covering the brain. Right underneath this area should be the juncture of the hemispherical fissure with the central fissure. Sort of a widening at the crossroads. That is where we will implant the bit of your own brain tissue that we saved from your operation." He motioned again to the nurse, and she wheeled up the glass culture tank which contained my transplant material. I looked at it with awe and respect. I did not recognize it as any part of me, brain or otherwise. And it did not really look as though it was living matter. It wasn't pulsing or bubbling or breathing, or anything like that. I couldn't see any blood vessels in it—not even capillaries. It looked to be a blob of irregular pale yellow jelly.

And now Virgil's meninges were cut, and Brother Tien was estimating the size and shape of her cranial fissure. He made up his mind instantly. He fished into the culture tank with a forceps, drew out my bit of tissue, and began to carve it with scissors and scalpel. When he had something that satisfied him, he dropped it into the hole in her head. He pulled it out once, took a snip at one edge, then dropped it in again. I could not see his mouth, but I could tell that he was smiling. It must have been a perfect fit.

"Close up," he told the nurse.

I heaved a sigh of relief.

Virgil's anesthetic wore off during the afternoon, and after that she was hellishly sick. She tried to vomit, but there was nothing in her stomach. She scraped at the bandages a little, but finally she just gave up and lay on her pallet, bleary eyed and panting.

"She's recovering nicely," Tien assured me. "Very strong heartbeat, good respiration. Can you 'read' anything?"

"Just fuzzy snatches, meaningless. No images. No words."

"About as expected. Let's leave her alone for the time being. We can look in on her tomorrow morning. Central will keep a visue-monitor on her meanwhile."

"You go on, Brother. I will stay with her."

He smiled. "As you wish. I will have the nurse bring you a cot."

In the early morning hours I heard a stirring behind the bars of Virgil's pen. I raised from the cot on an elbow and looked over. I could see her, standing motionless, glaring through the bars at me. And now she was making words, slowly, painfully, one at a time.

"You...great...lump...of...goat...dung."

I sat bolt upright. I fought a sudden impulse to open her cage and hug her around her beautiful neck. But better sense prevailed. "How do you feel, Virgil?" I asked politely.

"Let...out." She let me see a vision of a rabbit bounding ahead of her, twisting and turning. And the final leap. Next, she was up on a hilltop. It was night, very dark, and she was howling. It was a prolonged, eerie sound. It made my flesh creep. From somewhere in the distance there was an answering cry.

I focussed slowly, carefully, inside her brain, and began forming sentences there. "You want to go back home, of course. I don't blame you. Well, you can. I will take you. But first, Virgil, you must do something for me. I need your help."

"Why do you call me Virgil?"

"There was once a great prophet, Dante Alighieri, who visited a great and terrible underground city, and a man named Virgil was his guide."

"You're crazy. I'm no man. I'm no guide, and I've never been underground."

"You'll learn as we go along, Virgil. Accept it."

"Forget it."

"Then you will live and die in a cage."

She was silent a moment. The little piece of my cerebral cortex had introduced an unaccustomed element of logic in her mental process. She required extra time to deal with it. "You would do that to me?"

"Yes."

"Even though I have done you no harm?"

"Yes. You have to understand, Virgil, that I am willing to cause a great many people much trouble, pain, and inconvenience just to rescue my wife." I gave her a mental step-by-step scenario of how Beatra and I had gone to the cliff edge to see the gods-eye, and how the undergrounders had appeared, and how I had been shot, and how Beatra had been carried away. I explained the darkness that awaited us underground, and how I would need her eyes in my attempt to rescue Beatra.

She thought about all this for several minutes. Finally she said: "This Beatra, is she pretty?"

"You know she is."

"But there are lots of other pretty females around."

"None of them are Beatra."

She made an extraordinary statement. "You are going underground to find a woman who is probably dead. And even if she is alive, you will be dead before you get within twenty miles of her. And even if you find her, you will never get her out. You are not a brave man. You are simply a very stupid man. I am cursed forever to carry the brain tissue of a fool."

It was my own bit of brain speaking in her!

I said: "You will not help me?"

"No."

I got up and turned to go. My hand was on the door

when she whimpered. "Jeremy."

"Well?"

"You are not going to leave me here?"

"As soon as you are completely well, you will be placed in a zoo. You will be fed scraps of slaughtered cattle, and children will come to see you on Sundays and they will point at you."

"Suppose I went with you, and led you around in the dark. What else would I be expected to do?"

"When we are hiding, you will have to keep watch. Also, your ears are sharper than mine, and so is your sense of smell, not to mention your teeth. You may have to kill a few people."

"*We* will be killed."

I took a step toward the door.

"I will go with you," she said.

I smiled. "Virgil, you are thinking that as soon as we get into the open, you can break away and head for the woods, killing me first if necessary. Well, my lovely friend, forget it. We will never be in the open. You and I will be dropped into the surf that faces a long line of cliffs. In these cliffs are caves, called The Grottoes, that can be entered at low tide. If the sea crocodiles don't get us, we should be able to swim into one of the grottoes, climb up somewhere inside, and find our way down, down, down... into the bowels of the earth. You will never have a chance to make a run for it. You have to go down with me, help me find Beatra, then return with me. After that, I will take you back to your valley and release you."

"I will go, but I don't promise I won't try to escape."

"Nor would I believe you if you did promise."

10. An Early Rising

It was early in the morning, a few days later, while I was still in temporary quarters in one of the monastery cells near the animal pens, that I was awakened by a brisk pounding on my door.

"Enter," I called out groggily. I sat up on the edge of the bed. "Ah, Brother Tien?"

We both slipped into telepathic communication. It was faster and less ambiguous.

"I am here," said the Friar, "because we think you do not have much time. The wolf is not completely ready, and you really should have additional vortectic training. It is regrettable."

It was cold dawn, and I was still rubbing the sleep from my eyes. But I was awake enough to be instantly alarmed.

"Beatra? Is she in greater danger?"

"We have no knowledge of her, and no way to obtain any. You must know that. It's you we're thinking of, and your vortectic powers in particular."

"What's wrong?"

"We have reason to believe that your vortectic powers will soon vanish. Obviously, any attempt to rescue your wife must be undertaken while you are in full possession of your powers."

"Why didn't you tell me this sooner?"

"We learned it only an hour ago from Father Phaedrus. His time is upon him."

I understood. Phaedrus was dying and had begun to prophesy. And he must have said something about me. "How long do I have?"

"Please wait," he said. "First, I want to explain something." He pulled out a map. "Look at this."

I studied the map. I recognized the shoreline, New Bollamer, Horseshoe Bay, and other local points. Somewhat to the south, in northern Ginia, perhaps a dozen miles from the coast, was a point surrounded by wavering concentric circles. I estimated the circumferences to be roughly a mile apart.

"The circles," said the physician-monk, "are lines of equal vortectic strength, as measured by the actual weights of a pebble vortex that a given Brother has been able to lift. Mile by mile, as we come inward toward this point"—he indicated the center of the circles—"our strength increases, and it is greatest directly over the center area. We speculate that there is something underground there, some great radiating force, that supplies the energy that we use for our little tricks. Perhaps it's the same mysterious power source that fluoresces their wall pigments and lights their city." He rolled the map up. "But what it is, or how it works, we haven't the vaguest concept." He looked at me, and saw that I was attending carefully. "This power source, whatever it may be, has had, we think, three quite remarkable external consequences. Firstly, it is accelerating the earth's precession, which is to say, the conical revolution of the axis of rotation. Before the Desolation, the earth's axis pointed almost at Polaris. Owing to precession, the axis direction was moving in a slow circle toward Vega, in the constellation of Lyra. Normally, we would need another nine thousand years to reach the Vega orientation. But this great underground force has speeded up the sweep, and we are now already into Lyra. Secondly, the force is slowing the daily rotation of the earth. The earth now needs almost exactly three hundred and sixty days for a complete revolution around the sun. Before the Desolation, it was three hundred sixty-five plus. Thirdly, the temblors and earthquakes are milder here than at any other locale on the eastern seaboard. They are very likely held in check by this same strange force."

The concepts of earthquakes and precession and slowing the year to three hundred and sixty days I did not completely understand, nor did I see that they had anything to do with my approaching journey. But the essential thing was all too clear. Our vortectic powers were derived from a great energy source, far underground, and it would soon cease to function.

He said, "And so you ask, how long do you have. Let us consider. The Year of the Gray Snow yields to the Year of the Wolf, and the Year of the Wolf yields to the Year of the Green Leaves. It has long been prophesied, my son Jeremy, that the Brothers must lose their vortex powers in a Year of the Wolf."

Tomorrow was the last day of the Year of the Wolf.

I had twenty-four hours within which to go underground, find Beatra in a dark and evil city, and bring her out again.

I looked up at him thoughtfully. "Do I bring her out safe?"

His mind shield slammed down tight.

It was chilling.

"Very well," I said. "But I don't think I can face my Grandfather. Can you tell him?"

"Yes."

"And tell the abbot and Father Phaedrus farewell."

"You can do that yourself. Father Phaedrus requires that you see him before you go. And Abbot Arcrite is even now preparing the floater. He will take you on the first leg of your journey. For this reason he cannot attend the death ceremony."

"And yet it is permitted for me? I thought only the Brothers were admitted to the deathbed of another Brother."

"You are a very special case. Phaedrus wishes it. You must come."

"Well, of course."

11. MINDS WITHIN MINDS

A FEW MOMENTS later Brother Tien and I were admitted into the dimly lit death chamber.

It was a preselected place, special for the occasion. Many of Phaedrus' predecessors had likewise given up their spirits here. The room was large, high ceilinged (to permit ready escape of the soul), and heavy with incense.

The Brothers were kneeling in sorrowing semicircular rows around the bed. They had been chanting in low harmonious tones when I entered, but now they ceased, and were silent.

In the center of the bed lay the dying monk, covered to his neck by a light white blanket. His body was a bare skeleton, his skull hairless and glinting under the faint multicolored lights.

But he still lived. He was conscious, and his mind was still alert.

Something awesome was taking place. I felt nearly overwhelmed.

"Jeremy Wolfhead..."

I started, and took a step closer. The monks made way for me. "Yes, father?" I found that I was talking orally. But to him it did not matter.

"Within a very little while I shall prophesy, and then I shall die."

"Live forever, father."

"No time to be silly, my son."

"Sorry, father. I attend."

"Long ago I entered the mind of the Returner. I took all that he had. Did you know that? That was how we are able to tell you much about the world below."

"I see."

"Concentrate, Jeremy, enter in, and I will let you meet the Returner."

I tried to concentrate. For a moment, nothing much seemed to happen.

I relaxed, breathing quietly and rhythmically.

There was an image, then another.

I was in the mind of a stranger . . . a young man.

At first it was a haunting, tantalizing thing. But after a time I sensed the subsonic chords of terror.

Flecks and foam of memory washed past. Occasionally something would seem to catch, and lie against this mind, like a leaf drifting downstream and lodging against some submerged obstruction.

One sequence recurred again and again. The Returner was in a floater, cruising out over the bay, perhaps a hundred feet over the water. He was curious, and he was going to investigate something. During the last several months a series of hummocks (ten or eleven?) had materialized on field and forest, in a straight line that seemed to point to the grottoes of Horseshoe Bay.

He had inspected several of those hummocks. He knew they were great piles of rock *cuttings*. He knew this meant subterranean excavations. Something or someone was carving out a tunnel far underground, and somehow was transporting the rock topside. By now the tunnel must have reached an exit in one of the grottoes.

An underground civilization? He knew the myths, the fireside fairy tales taught in childhood. He remembered the strange prophecies handed down by the Brothers. It is the Year of the Wolf. Hell and its leaders are about to burst forth and kill every living thing on the surface. But they are thwarted just in time when a hero descends into their dark caverns, swims their terrible river Lethe, slays their monsters, and finally destroys their city.

Perhaps he was the one.

Then the memories returned, and he screamed. (But it was not a human sound, because of what they had done to him.)

The Returner remembered.

The sun was bright, the water quiet. The grottoes beckoned.

Which one to try first?

The biggest. That great sea cave, there. He brought the vessel down at the entrance to the great grotto and hovered there. Inside the sea cave all was dark and silent. The only sound was the rhythmic rush of the surf into the cave. Slowly he inched forward, keeping plenty of room above and below the craft. There were sea crocodiles hereabouts, and this would be a most inconvenient place to strike a jutting rock and disable his ship.

He turned on the beams and drifted inward a dozen yards or so. The lights showed that the cave side on his left came down in a steep wall to meet the sea. On the right, however, was a shallow shore, a jumble of rocks, sand, and gravel, that seemed to continue back into the cave for a considerable distance.

He cruised slowly on, looking for a better place to put the craft down. But the shelf didn't really get any better. In fact, it began to narrow. He would have to stop soon, if he were going to be able to turn the ship around. He picked out a barely possible patch on the shore and headed the ship toward it.

Then, all around him, the world seemed to explode. The little ship dropped on the rocks and broke up in flames. He stumbled out. Something hit him in the shoulder, and he dropped, paralyzed. Perhaps he was hit again. The Returner couldn't remember.

Time passed for the Returner. He had a dim awareness of figures standing around him. Strange men, with big eyes. They could see in the dark. Or did he find that out later? They tied him up, put him on a stretcher, and set off with him in the darkness.

And now the gaps began. And the images were too blurred to grasp. Much time and darkness had passed, and the Returner was still underground.

In the final sequence he was listening to voices. He was afraid.

The one they called the President said: "There will be others. We must give them warning, never to attempt to enter here."

"Then we should kill this one," said someone.

"They would never know, then, would they?" said the President. "We lose the possibility of making him serve as a warning."

"But if we release him, he will tell them all that he has seen here."

"Not necessarily. I am thinking of a silent warning. He will be silent, yet he will represent a living warning as to what will happen to others who attempt to enter our city. We will give to him, and to all who might try to follow him, the Vow of Silence."

I, Jeremy Wolfhead (I had to search for my own identity for a moment!) jerked with pain. I was sweating copiously. I did not want to know about the Vow of Silence.

But I had to know. I re-entered the dying mind of Phaedrus, and within it the mind of The Returner.

The Returner himself seemed to answer. He was

mind-speaking, long ago, to the abbot. I listened with Phaedrus. "The Vow of Silence? They cut out my tongue and sewed up my lips. But I got away. I took a floater. Down the great river. Over the falls, then down, down, down. Then the exploding heat, and steam, and up, up, up, tumbling and whirling. And now you must let me die. It is my right." (I knew that I was hearing again a plea made to the abbot twenty years ago. And next I heard the abbot's reply.)

"Nay, friend-who-returns. We are the Brothers. Your floater fell out of the Spume and into the snow dune. That is why you still live. Your body is broken and your mind is hurt. But it is our business to mend broken bodies. And we can help your mind to recover. You will live."

"No."

"You have parents. You have a wife. She carries your child. They need you. They think only of you. They are still sending out search parties. You should let us tell them."

"No. Tell them nothing. I am going to die. It is best that they think I am dead."

It was bewildering and horrifying.

Why was Phaedrus showing this to me?

"You have not understood everything," Phaedrus murmured wearily within my mind. "And perhaps I do not blame you. And indeed, it may be for the best. For when the time comes that you do understand—and that time must come—your sudden frenzy will give you added strength. You will become a momentary madman. Nevertheless, I must leave matters of the past and of the present."

I was crushed. I had concentrated, I had done my very best to follow the images, and it had been for nothing. I had failed him.

He said softly: "I prophesy."

The chamber was deathly silent.

The play of minds within minds had cost him much.

He had faded greatly. The thoughts ebbed, waned. I barely caught them.

He continued faintly. "All the generations of the Brotherhood have existed but to send you underground at this hour. It is effort well spent. The Brothers are worthy, and you are worthy. The millennia have finally brought forth this day, these twenty-four hours. And in the last of these hours it will be decided that one great culture will live and one will die. Beware..." His voice died away.

I waited a moment, then I said, "Beware *what*, father?"

"The gods-eye."

I felt childishly at fault again, for I could not fathom what he was talking about. What cultures did he mean? And how, being underground, would I have any control over the gods-eye, which was far overhead? But at any rate, while he was prophesying, I would put to him the question that meant the most to me. "Do I bring Beatra out again?"

"Yes." (A thought-wisp, so faint I barely caught it.)

"Safe?"

I realized instantly that my earlier question should have been, "Do I bring her out safe?" But it was too late. The flickering fire in his mind had gone out. He was dead. And the chanting had already begun again.

I seemed to hear fluttering echoes of his mind-voice. "Jeremy, my son,... my son... my son..."

I was wracked by sudden chills; the funeral scars on my chest throbbed.

I barely noted the little white bird that came from nowhere, circled the room once, then soared up toward the high ceiling and disappeared.

I was turning to look for Brother Tien, when a hand touched my shoulder. It was he. Briefly I studied the face of the physician-monk. I knew he loved Phaedrus, not only as surrogate-father, but also as a product of his great surgical skill. Phaedrus' death must be taking a heavy toll on the sensibilities of this good man.

But his face was a carven mask. It showed nothing of his feelings. I wanted to say something to him, something to tell him I understood his grief, just a few bright and banal cliché sentences, but it was no good. "Sorry," I muttered.

"It was best," he said gently. "His time had come." There was not the slightest tremor in his voice. "Are you ready?"

I thought of Grandfather. After he got over the initial shock of my departure, he would probably organize another funeral and lay another empty coffin in the earth alongside Beatra's.

I sighed, then turned as Brother Tien spoke again. "Our abbot waits for you in the floater. You must hurry."

"Virgil?" I asked.

"She is on board. Goodbye, Jeremy."

"Yes, my friend."

I never saw him again.

12. THE GATES OF HELL

ABBOT ARCRITE TOOK the helm of my floater (which he promised to return to my grandfather), and we set off across Horseshoe Bay to the distant grottoes. I looked down at Virgil from time to time. She trembled and whimpered most of the way out. What behavior for a dire wolf—the king of the forest!

After a time the face of the great cliffs loomed large, and the abbot let the floater sink low over the waves. "This," he said, "is as close as I dare to bring the floater. The undergrounders have detection devices at the mouth of the grotto. We know this from the report of the Returner."

Always this shadowy figure. Captured by the undergrounders, his brain drained away from him, and given the Vow of Silence. But, as I knew from my vivid encounter with the dying Phaedrus, he had escaped, and had been brought back to a brief demilife by the Brothers. The Vow of Silence—which simply involved cutting out his tongue and lacing up his lips—did not prevent telepathic communication with him. But all of that was many years ago, and there was no way to know whether the things the Brothers had learned from him were still true.

I took a last look up at the lightening sky. There was a faint red in the north, and far overhead a V of wild swans was awing. But the V was inverted, with the apex to the rear. Also, just over the southern horizon, the gods-eye, the symbol of all my past misfortunes and perhaps the harbinger of even worse to come, was about to vanish below the sea rim. I shivered. All the auguries were bad.

I looked over the railing down through the dim dawnlight into the waves. The wind had come up and there was a pounding surf under us.

"What are we about to do?" asked Virgil nervously.

"Do you see that big cave in the cliff—just at shore level?"

"Yes."

"Well, we're going to dive in and swim over there."

"If you think I am going to jump into all that cold wet water," said Virgil, "you are an idiot."

"Can you lower the floater a few feet?" I asked the abbot.

He obliged me, checking his height from time to time. "I can't get too close. If a wave hits us we will be knocked into the water." But he got us within about six feet, and that was good enough. "Hurry," he said.

I stripped quietly, put my dagger between my teeth, and blanked out my mind. Virgil looked up at me instantly, but before she could realize what I was up to, I had lifted her in my arms and had jumped over the railing. I felt a snarl in my brain as we went over. We landed with a great *plosh*, went under, then struggled back up to the surface. I looked up in the semidarkness, but the floater was already pulling up and away. The abbot waved at me, but I did not wave back. The past was gone, and he had gone with it. It seemed now that the sun-world was no longer relevant. Like Brother

Tien, the abbot had now passed out of my life forever.

Virgil had gathered sufficient of her wits about her to begin treading water and to curse me in nuances of lupo-human vocabulary I had not thought possible. I took her reaction as a good sign, and began swimming toward the largest of the caves. From time to time I waited for her to catch up. Once, when I thought she was tiring, I let her rest with her forepaws on my back. We caught our breath for several minutes before attempting to pass through the last and worst of the surf. One of the breakers separated us, and once I saw her a couple of yards away struggling upside down, with her legs clawing at the air. When she finally straightened out she had much to say, but by then we were working our way into the great grotto.

I thought our troubles with the water were over. I was wrong. A great sinuous shape lashed the water near Virgil. I took my blade in hand and dove to her rescue. The sea creature was at that moment giving all of his attention to her flashing jaws and did not notice until it was far too late that I was under him and was busily cutting his throat. He turned on me, but I was too quick for him. He died in the murk of his own blood.

And now I thought of the abbot's warning. "Have nothing dead on you when you enter the grotto. No clothing, metal, stone, or wood. Only living matter can enter the grottoes without detection." With vast regret, I threw the knife away.

The next breaker swept both wolf and man into the gloomy interior of the cave, where we managed to haul ourselves up on the slimy rocks.

Virgil sniffed once at me. She didn't like the blood-odor. "Think of it as a big sea rabbit," I said.

As we lay there panting and slowly regaining our strength, I looked around me in the near-darkness. There was barely enough light from the mouth of the cave to illuminate the grotto for a few yards behind us.

Beyond that there was a weird green phosphorescence. The abbot had prepared me for this. This flickering ghost light emanated from the myriad bodies of tiny sea microbes, in the water, on the moist surfaces of the rocks, and up the walls and even on the ceilings. It had nothing to do with the fluorescent pigment the undergrounders used in some of their streets and caverns.

Just ahead of us, crumpled on the rocks, lay the charred skeleton of what had evidently once been a floater. How long had it been here? What foolhardy soul had brought it here? Could it have been the Returner? Had he cruised in at low tide, his curiosity overriding his good sense, and had he got shot down by some invisible detecto-gun?

I looked overhead. Sure enough, I thought I could see there the glint of glass and metal. The killing beam. He had been lucky to escape with his life.

As I passed around the bow of the hulk, I noticed the figurehead, or rather what once had been the figurehead. But it was now too charred to recognize. It was the head of something or someone, but beyond that, it would be hard even to speculate.

We passed on.

Then Virgil stopped suddenly and stood there, still as a rock, her hackles raised. She was staring into the depths of the cave.

"What is it?" I signaled to her.

"I don't know, but I don't like it. And incidentally, there are several of them."

"Let's go take a look," I said.

"You go first."

I stood up and started picking my way over the rocks toward the rear of the cave.

"You make enough noise," she said. "Why don't you cry out to let them know we are coming?"

For the next few minutes I tried to be quiet, but I stumbled around a bit all the same.

Then I heard it, something heavy, lumbering, something slithery. We both stopped and froze.

Then came the bellow.

"It's a croc," I flashed to her.

She moved out a few steps ahead of me, and a horrible growl rumbled deep in her throat.

I warned her instantly: "Get back here, you nitwit!"

Now I could actually see the dark outline of the beast. It was a good ten yards long. Virgil and I together would hardly make a good appetizer.

I had no weapon. It was immaterial anyhow because I did not think anything smaller than an electrocannon would have much effect on this leviathan. Still...I noted that where the walls came down to the grotto floor, pockets of sand had collected. This was all I needed. I willed that one pinch of sand levitate, then another to balance it, and soon I had a whirling disc in motion. And now time seemed to stand still.

"There are three more behind him," signaled Virgil.

My sand disc struck him in the right eye, then I whipped it over, and it took out his left eye. He came on for a moment even so, and then he began to scream. He dived into the water not two yards distant from us, and for a moment there was a great churning. One by one the other creatures hurried after him into the water.

I noted then that sweat was streaming down my face, and I was cold. Virgil looked up at me with a grudging respect.

We pushed on into the deepening gloom. The finger of the sea soon disappeared, and we were walking on damp sand. The cave corridor began to widen perceptibly, and then we stood before a fork in the cave. Without hesitation I said, "Let's take the right-hand fork."

"You are pretty sure of yourself," she said.

Near-darkness faded into total darkness. Should I form a light-ball? Did they have sentries here, or light detectors? I decided to play it safe for the time being.

We walked on for perhaps a hundred yards, Virgil slightly ahead of me. Suddenly she stopped and I almost fell over her.

My mind whispered to hers, "What's wrong?"

"There is some kind of chasm here."

I got down on my hands and knees and crawled inch by inch, and sure enough there it was. I felt around for a pebble and tossed it over the edge. We both listened intently for a long time.

"Didn't you hear it?" I asked her.

"I heard nothing," she said. "We might as well go home now."

"No, we take the other fork."

We made our way back to the fork and took the left turn this time.

Within a few minutes we were stopped again. This time we were clearly on the right path. We had encountered a human artifact—the product of what had to be an advanced culture. There was an enormous iron grid across the tunnel face. I tried to rattle it but it would not budge. In the near-darkness I felt the bars. Each was at least an inch in diameter, and they crisscrossed on two-inch centers. Only very small creatures could work themselves through the grid openings.

I now realized that all manner of gates, doors, and portals were scattered within and without the city, all aimed at protecting vital parts of the dark metropolis, all locked, barred, and closed against intruders such as me. Probably no two were alike, and each successive door would present a new challenge and new demands on my skills. And perhaps I would finally find one I could not open, and that would be the end of me and Beatra. But that possibility I wouldn't even consider. Opening this one would not lead me directly to her. At most, it might give me license to search out the rest of the doors. In any way that I examined the problem, all answers started with opening this great grid.

Virgil looked up at me. "*Now* can we go home?"

13. Beyond the Iron Gate

"Can you see anything?" I asked.

She peered through the great grid. "There is something big in there, covered with something, perhaps some sort of cloth. It hangs loosely over the thing."

"Canvas?"

"I don't know about canvas. But I guess it could be."

"Is it a floater?"

Her nose twitched. "Perhaps."

It had to be a floater. It must be the same one that had taken Beatra. And that meant there had to be some way to raise this grid. There should be some machinery inside, and a switch to activate it.

I knew that I could in time cut through the bars with a spinning sand disc. But that would certainly tell these people that I had entered the cavern, and for the time being I did not want them to know I was here.

There had to be another way.

I listened. There was nothing. Even the crashing surf was lost at this distance.

I had to chance it. I formed a ball of light on the other side of the grid and moved it slowly around the walls and ceiling near the gate. I found what I knew had to be there: a hydraulic lift mechanism, complete with electric servo-motor. Two parallel wires ran from the motor to a panel box fixed in the cave side. I could barely make out a keyhole in the panel door. It was locked, of course.

I had to speculate about the mechanism inside the panel box. Presumably there was a permabattery, and next to that, a switch. When you closed the switch, the current flowed, the motor ran, and the gate lifted.

The only difficulty was, I couldn't think of any way to get into the panel box to close the switch.

But then I remembered an experiment I had carried out during my vortectic training. It would not be necessary to get into the panel box.

I brought the luminous vortex over to the wire pair where they emerged from the panel box, and let it hang there. Then I formed a cylindrical vortex, with just enough diameter to let the periphery impinge on one of the wires, and I doubled, quadrupled, its rate of spin. And the wire began to turn color. It soon became red hot in the vortex area and began to emit a faint light of its own. Electrons were flowing from the hot end to the cold end. Despite the open switch, an electric current was being generated in the circuit.

There was a sudden click as the servo-motor turned on. The gate rolled slowly up into its ceiling receptacle.

But then a soft red light began to blink overhead, just inside. That wasn't so good. An alarm had been sent somewhere.

I collapsed the vortices and jumped inside. Virgil followed.

After a moment the gate cranked down again, evidently moving by simple gravity. The red light went off. The darkness was total.

Just then the tunnel floor began to vibrate. The

great gate rattled metallically in its guide channels.
Virgil whined and ran over to my side. "What is
happening?" she asked.

I swallowed. "I am not really sure. Perhaps it is
heavy machinery somewhere." I thought I knew what it
was, but I did not want her to know. Not yet. "In any
case, it seems to have stopped." Which it had. The
tunnel was quiet again.

I peered down the corridor, but it was totally dark,
and I could see nothing. I dared not reform the light-
ball, because I suspected we would have visitors
shortly.

"Anything moving down there?" I asked Virgil.

"I can't see anything. There are man smells, but they
are old."

We moved slowly in the darkness. I reached out and
touched the canvas on the big object. I felt the floater
hull underneath.

Virgil stopped suddenly. "I hear footsteps. Men
running this way."

"How many?"

"Two, I think."

"They will have weapons," I said. "We will have to
hide."

"Where?"

"In the floater. Under the canvas."

"That will be the first place they search."

Even my dull human ears now picked up the sound
of padding feet. "I know. Come on." I lifted her up, and
in a moment we were well hidden under the folds.

We could hear them clearly now. Two men,
running, with sure even strides. And here they were,
right upon us. They stopped, panting, and looked
around.

"Nobody here," said one.

He spoke with a strange accent, but I understood
him perfectly.

"But the gate went up," said the other. "The switch

can only be opened and closed from the inside."

"But we had a temblor a few minutes ago. It was severe enough to momentarily short-circuit the switch. See, the panel box is still locked. It was just a false alarm."

"You may be right. But even so, we had better check the floater. The corporal will certainly ask about the floater."

While they were talking, I had been trying to see out through a partially open fold in the canvas. I saw the barest patch of light. The men were using some sort of portobeam.

Virgil might now be required to kill a man, quickly and cleanly, and with absolutely no hesitation. I thought of Goro, the hound. He had hesitated, and he had died. Even though—like Goro—she was not bred to kill human beings, Virgil had an inherent advantage. She hated humanity. Probably even me. I was certain she would perform adequately.

"They are going to pull back the canvas from this side," I signaled to her. "You take the one next to you, and I'll take the other. Go for the throat."

"The throat? My goodness!" There was a sarcastic sneer in her assent, as though I, a mere human, were instructing her in the art of stalking woodchucks.

An unseen hand flipped back the heavy cloth.

Virgil struck. There was a crack as the portobeam struck the cavern floor and shattered.

I grappled in the darkness with the other guard. One of my hands found a weapon, the other his throat. He went over backward into the sand and rocks, and we rolled over and over. He was a big man, considerably taller and heavier than I, and despite my initial advantage of surprise, I was unable to wrest his gun from him or do him any real damage. And soon, owing to his greater strength, he began slowly to twist his weapon toward me. We were locked side by side in lethal embrace, both of us grunting and panting, and the nose of his weapon was moving in tiny shuddering arcs toward my head. But these few split seconds of immobility gave me time to form a sand vortex, as a thin, whining disc. It formed just over his head, and I brought it down into his skull, just over his ear. Particles of bloody bone splattered all over my face. His body relaxed instantly. I got up and looked for Virgil. I could see nothing. "Virgil?" I called softly.

I could hear her footsteps sauntering over toward me. She yawned cavernously. "I thought I might have to help you."

I dusted the sand off my chest and legs. "Any trouble?"

"His throat was very soft. The jugular and windpipe came out together. He dropped, twitched a little, and there he is."

"Thank you."

There was the suggestion of a shrug in her reply. "If I let you get killed, how do I get out?"

"You have a point." I made a light-ball and studied the face of the man I had killed. So violent in life, so peaceful in death. The pale features were completely relaxed, the mouth curling in a half-smile, the great owl-eyes languidly half-open. He was a little older than I. Perhaps a kind husband and a loving father. I did not want to inspect Virgil's victim, but I had the almost certain impression that he was a young man, still a boy. His mother would mourn him tonight. They had both been doing their duty, and we had cut them down.

But I did not permit myself to feel sorry for either of them. They would have been quite happy to have killed us. They—and all their kind—were my deadly enemies.

I turned back to the body of "my" man and began stripping off his uniform. The fabric of the uniform was soft and subtle, closely woven from some light, synthetic monofilamentary material. Some of our own fabrics were of course machine woven, but they did not compare with this stuff.

Virgil watched in patient disapproval while I fastened his sandals on my feet and checked his electropistol. It was neither better nor worse than similar electros I had restored in our family shops. How odd that these people, with such advantages, had stood still, technology-wise, for thirty centuries.

I holstered the pistol and picked up the weapon of the other guard. "And now," I said, "we have to get out of here. Stay just ahead of me as we go down the tunnel."

So then, on our first encounter, we had come off fairly well. But it was just the beginning, and the odds were still great against us. For they had preserved all their culture, their science and technology, and they had been at the peak of their civilization just before Desolation struck. And I was only one man—by their standards an illiterate savage and half-blind. I dared not openly inquire for information concerning Beatra. I dared not even show myself openly to any of them. During the coming hours I could only operate by stealth and low cunning. And perhaps I would have to leave a trail of corpses behind me. Well, despite the odds, and despite their technology, I was determined to beat them. I would defeat their guards, their President, and the entire dark, dank city of Dis, and I would escape with Beatra.

We went on, ever downward. I followed the sound of Virgil's footsteps, steady, yet cautious. We soon entered an area where phosphorescent pigment had been applied to the walls, and I could see our surroundings, albeit very dimly.

We had now come half a mile, without a glimmer of real light. Nothing but this eerie dimness, where everything seemed half-hallucination. It troubled me. Would the entire underground be this dark? Yet, I couldn't complain. So far it was exactly as described by the Returner.

"Stop!" said Virgil.

I waited while she sniffed the air. "For a moment the odors were quite strong. Now they are weaker. I think a door opened, then closed again."

"That might have been the corporal of the guard, looking out the door to see whether his two men are returning. Did you smell metal? Such as rifles stacked? Radios or communicators?"

"Many metals. Yes."

"Undoubtedly a guardpost, stuck right in the middle of the tunnel. How many men?"

"Two different scents."

"Can you see the door from here?"

"No. I think it may be around a bend of the tunnel, perhaps fifty yards away. We are very close."

I felt the floor of the corridor. Hard, almost glazed. Obviously artificially dug, possibly by some machine that chopped out pieces of stone with a white-hot cutting blade. And what did they do with the pieces? Perhaps they got some of them to the surface. The Returner had seen a line of hummocks, leading to the grotto area. Some of their excavation debris, on the other hand, they might well dump into pre-existing gorges, such as the one we had nearly stepped into. In cutting out their underground corridors they probably took advantage of natural caverns whenever they encountered them, such as the grotto caves in the cliff side.

It was great engineering, but it left the tunnel floor smooth as glass. No sand. No rubble. No pebbles. And I did not dare form a luminous sphere. No vortex for this place.

Nevertheless, I was going through that guardpost. Somehow. I had to. On the other side I could hope to find someone who would tell me where Beatra was being held. I needed information. I needed a feel for the area, the people. Very importantly, assuming I could actually find Beatra, I needed to know how to get her out again. The bodies at the grid gate must sooner or later be discovered, and when that happened, this exit would certainly be blockaded. Was there another way out? (Aside from the deadly Spume, which had served the Returner so brutally!)

I shook my head. Enough thinking! Another door stood in my way. Action was needed. Although there seemed no good way to use my vortectic powers, at least I had two electropistols. There was not enough light to aim them properly, but perhaps this could be remedied. It would require very accurate timing.

I said to Virgil, "The door is locked, of course. And there is a password, or a secret knock, or something to identify the returning patrolmen. We don't have it. Nevertheless, we have got to make them open that door without shooting us. We will move very quietly toward the door. I don't know whether it opens to the right or to the left. So I will have to stand back a little. And here's what I want you to do." I explained the plan carefully. An hour ago she might have protested that it was insane. For the time being, however, she seemed to have given up.

We found the door just around the bend. I stayed hidden while she trotted up to within a few yards of the door. And then she lay down and began to whimper and whine.

14. The Guardhouse

In a few seconds I heard a creak. Although I could see nothing, I knew the door was opening a little. I knew that curious eyes were peering out through the slit. I heard a muffled exclamation. The man had seen Virgil. And now the door creaked again. He had evidently called his companion. Presumably two heads were now thrust through the door space. There was probably at least one gun drawn on her. Now there was a hurried whispered conference. I heard a muffled dialog but could not distinguish any individual words.

My moment had come. I stepped around the bend, brought both pistols up, aiming at what I supposed were the two theoretical heads in a theoretical doorway. I pulled the triggers. Flickering blue-white beams of light shot out. And I saw both guards in that instant. I had actually hit one of them. The guard on my left. The shot struck him in the neck and killed him almost instantly. The other shot struck the door and knocked a hole in it. But it did not matter. I got off another shot from the pistol in my right hand, so quickly that the two men seemed to fall together.

Virgil got up and came over to sniff at them. She coughed. "That thing makes a bad smell, and it makes a smelly hole."

"The beam makes a lot of ozone. The gas has a bitter scent, and it can make you cough. The smell in the wounds is simply burnt flesh. You must have seen the same thing when you hunted with old Thornhouse."

"Yes, I remember." She was thoughtful. "That was all very long ago, wasn't it? And then you did this... thing to me. I am not the same. I don't know what I am anymore."

"It was done, and here we are. We should not have to renegotiate our contract every hundred yards. Live with it, Virgil. Especially since we now have to figure out what we do next."

"Yes, great hunter."

I pulled the two bodies outside into the tunnel. Then we stepped cautiously into the guardhouse. I closed the door behind us and felt around in the darkness. I found a desk and chair. I dropped into the chair. I heard sounds suggesting that Virgil was snuffing about the room. "You can see me easily," I said. "You can see everything here. But I can barely make you out. It is too dark. I need to see through your eyes."

"You can."

"What do you mean, I can?"

"You always could. But I have never let you. I am entitled to my privacy."

"How is this done?"

"If I choose to do it."

"If you choose to do it."

"Start with the present situation. You have implanted a little piece of your brain at a certain place in my brain. It has developed contact with certain knowledge and judgment centers of my brain. If I determine a fact, it is passed on to this bit of foreign matter within my skull. And this occurs whether I like it or not. And then you can ask this bit of you within me, is it dark, or is it light, or is someone coming, or what do you hear, and it answers you back. But in substance, you are talking to me through your ambassador, and not to my senses directly."

"And you now say I can see directly with your eyes? I don't have to ask, 'Do you see anyone coming?'"

"That is true."

"Why didn't you tell me this before?"

"Because it was none of your business."

"But now, you have changed your mind?"

"I am thinking about it."

I knew better than to press her. "Well, Virgil, think about it. Meanwhile we have to plan the next stage of the search. We have to get a general idea of the street plan of this underground city. We have to capture a local citizen and ask him where Beatra is being kept. Then we have to go there, free her, and escape."

"It sounds very simple."

I knew she was being sarcastic. I asked, "Can you see anything on the walls? There ought to be a map of the city in a guardpost."

She got up and walked around the room and halted at the opposite wall. "There is something here. Full of crisscrossing lines."

I felt my way over, knocking over a chair in the process. It was a rather large panel, head tall, and wide as my outspread arms. But all I could see was a gross mass of gray. I needed a light, but dared not make a luminous globe.

I felt along the wall area near the two doors for some sort of switch. I couldn't find it. I could hear Virgil yawning. That meant she was bored and impatient. "What you are looking for isn't there."

I tried the desks. Perhaps a portobeam? But why would they need one? It wasn't dark in here to these people. Well, did they smoke the bacco weed? Would I find a match, a lighter? I found nothing. I couldn't even find two sticks to rub together, whereby I have started a fire many times on hunting trips. Perhaps I would have to risk a luminous globe.

"We can go back," said Virgil. "All we have to do is go back through the tunnel, raise the gate, get in the floater, and off we go. They can't possibly stop you."

"Virgil, are we going to die here because you won't let me look at a map?"

"I could get out all by myself."

"Now who's crazy?"

"Well, I'm not your slave, you know. You could at least say please. If you want to see through my eyes, that is."

"Please."

And so I was permitted 'inside.' From my implanted cortical fragment I radiated slowly down a labyrinth of neural pathways to her optical lobe, the visual center at the back of her cerebral cortex. Her optical nerves terminated here, and around these termini were fixed the images of her entire visual history, both consciously and unconsciously remembered. Before I came to rest in the present, I passed through the meadows and forests that had formed her life in her glacial valley home with old trapper Thornhouse.

And so, with her eyes I looked about the guardroom. It was surprisingly large and roomy. The ceiling must have been fifteen feet high. And looking up, I saw something move: an odd sort of mobile dangling from the ceiling, and trembling. I was sure it wasn't there for esthetic purposes, but I couldn't imagine why it had been hung there. Another oddity: there was a small aquarium on a rack by one of the walls. In the bottom were two tiny things that looked like miniature catfish. Somehow, the patrolmen of Dis didn't strike me as keepers of pet fish. This aquarium, like the mobile, was here for a purpose.

Virgil was becoming impatient again. She closed her eyes, shutting off my vision. I took the hint. "The map, Virgil."

"The map, O great master."

If it pleased her, I could live with it.

She looked up at the wall, and saw the map. It was all in shades of white, brown, and gray. That surprised me. I had expected colors. But whether Virgil was color-blind, or the undergrounders were color-blind, or whether this was their usual way of making maps, there was no way to know. But for the moment it scarcely mattered. The plat was sufficiently confusing in this simple format. Initially, it was incomprehensible. Then streets, avenues, and buildings began to emerge. But the lettering was peculiar. Our own letters and alphabet had evidently diverged considerably during the three thousand years that the Desolation had separated us. What I needed was a starting point. I looked around the edges of the panel and finally found what I wanted. There was an arrow, pointing to a tiny square that sat on a curving line. There were three words over the arrow. I made them out to read, "You are here." I traced the line out to its end. There, in a different shade of brown, was drawn part of the contour of Horseshoe Bay. It showed the very cave where we had entered.

Starting there, I traced my way down the corridor to our present post, then down the tunnel toward the city, where it emerged into several forks opening on a square. I studied the network of crisscrossing lines. Perhaps here they did not have buildings in the sense that I knew them. Probably they had simply cut out rooms with their excavating equipment, leaving walls and archways as supports to hold up the overlying rocks.

Well, all of this speculation was futile. However the buildings were made, there were no labels on any of them. Nothing that said, 'Beatra Held Here,' or even 'Jail,' 'Police Station,' 'Hospital,' or anything like that.

I returned Virgil's vision to her, walked back behind the desk, and sat down. "We are going to have to do a little kidnaping of our own. We have to find someone who knows where Beatra is."

"Opportunity is about to knock," said Virgil dryly.

She heard it first, of course. And now I heard it—the sound of boots clomping up the corridor on the city side. Probably the patrol relief. Did they suspect anything? No, they couldn't.

I reached out for their minds. But it was a jumble, and they were not yet close enough for me. "How many?" I asked Virgil.

"Two."

It was to be expected. Periodically, they would relieve two men out of four. Was there a password? Perhaps there was no need for one on this side of the post. But just to make sure, I opened the "front" door casually, glanced toward the approaching men (whom I could see only vaguely), lifted my arm in brief greeting, and, leaving the door wide open, walked back into the office.

Virgil, whom I had commanded to hide under the desk, gave me her eyes again. I was leaning over the desk as they came in, apparently looking at some papers. But this was purely for appearances. All the while I was in Virgil's mind, watching them intently with her eyes.

The two men were about the same height, stocky, muscular, with stolid features. As expected, their eyes were large, and the pupils within them were the size of coins.

As they entered, I got up from the chair, turned away from them, and stretched, meanwhile watching them carefully through Virgil's eyes. Then I pulled the electrobeam from the holster at my belt and turned around. I spoke into their minds simultaneously. "Gentlemen, please do exactly as you are told, or I will kill you. First of all, drop your gun holsters. Easy, easy. Now, raise your hands."

They did as they were told, while their chins slowly dropped, and, if it were possible, their eyes widened further. The first to enter seemed to recover first. "Who are you!" he said hoarsely. "What is this!" Now their eyes began darting about the room. "Where is the patrol?" demanded the first man. His accent was odd, but I could understand him perfectly. And presumably he could understand me. I switched over to plain talk.

"I have killed the four men of the patrol."

"What do you want?" whispered Number One."

"Cooperation."

They waited, motionless, arms uplifted, wary. Meanwhile Virgil came out from under the clothes rack.

"Look at that!" gasped Number Two. They both took a step backward. Number One began to lower his right arm.

"Don't be stupid," I said. "If you tell me what I want to know, she will not touch you."

"And what do you want to know?"

"There is a floater in stocks at the terminus of this corridor, just before the grid-gate." I pointed to the map. "Four weeks ago one of your raiding parties took that floater, opened the gate, and crossed to the opposite point of the bay. There you killed my hound Goro, shot a piece out of my skull, left me for dead, and took away my wife, Beatra. I am here to take her back. All you have to do is tell me where I can find her."

Number One answered in a low, incredulous guttural: "You are mad!" But images were forming in his brain. *He knew. He had seen.* She had been taken to a house. A big, special place.

If he could only be persuaded to put it into words, it would crystallize, and I would have what I needed. I could make him do it, but a slight shift in tactics was indicated. I sighed and turned to Number Two. "Open the exit door over there and tell us what you see. Nothing sudden. Slow and easy."

He walked over, opened the door, and looked down the corridor. His voice came back as strained and twisted as the image in his mind. "Two bodies. Looks like Josson and Smit."

Through Virgil's eyes I studied Number Two. "If you refuse to assist me, there is no reason why I should permit you to continue to live."

"I don't really know anything," said the guard. "I know only what they say, that the President led a raid and captured a sun-devil female."

"Where is she?" I put the question to Number Two.

"I don't know." Sweat was pouring down his face. It was particularly odd, because by Virgil's infrared scan, his face was cold and clammy, and these streaks of perspiration were by comparison scalding hot. They showed up as brilliant, lacy streaks on his forehead and cheeks.

"What have you heard?"

Number Two sneaked an uneasy glance at his companion. Number One frowned at him. The frown was wasted, for Number Two truly knew nothing specific. But he was about to have a profound influence on Number One, who *did* know something.

I shot Number Two between the eyes. He was starting to fall before Number One understood what had happened.

"He refused to cooperate," I explained gently. "But I expect that you will have better sense."

Number Two crashed to the floor, and the sweat jumped from Number One's face. And now the words and images were forming quickly. "The White House," he stammered. "On the seventh level. You can find it easily. Take the descender to the second level. Proceed down the street half a mile through the warehouses, then take the next descender to the seventh level, and go on straight way to the White House. That's where she's being held."

"I want you to go over to the map, and draw a circle around this 'White House.'"

"With what?"

"You have a marker in your breast pocket."

"They will kill me!"

"Maybe not. But I certainly will, if you don't do as I suggest."

He stepped over the body of his fallen companion and faced the map. He drew a wavering circle around a cluster of interconnecting squares in the center of the panel.

And now I was satisfied that that was all he could tell me. I looked at him contemplatively. He grasped what I was thinking, and his arms jerked.

"Steady!" I warned him.

The problem was (and he well understood this), that if I tied him up the next relief would discover him in a few hours. Could I find Beatra and get her out in that time? How long would it take to find the White House? What further delays and dangers lay ahead? One call from this place, and the White House would be ringed with guards, and every patrol in the city would be on the streets searching for me. I could not leave him here. But I did not dare take him with me. Was there any undiscoverable nook or cranny nearby where I could leave him, safely bound and gagged for the time being?

The decision was taken from me.

The guard dropped and dove at my feet.

Unhappily for him, I was in his mind. I had followed the gathering of his resolve, the flow of impulses in his motor cranial areas, the tensing of his toes and leg muscles.

I shot him in the head and simultaneously stepped out of the way of his lunging corpse. I begrudged this second blue flash, but it couldn't be helped. Had the sudden light been noticed through the windows? I opened the door for Virgil. She looked down the corridor on the city side, sniffing curiously. "Nothing, nobody. Just some very interesting smells."

I looked through her eyes. It was a fairly wide street, even though it was evidently in a little-frequented part of the city. But there was something very strange about it: it was lined on both sides with floaters. Empty, waiting...? Waiting for what? A puzzle! Beyond the lines of floaters seemed to be blank walls interspersed with doors. Storage and tool sheds, I hazarded. All very curious, but I had no time to sort it out.

"Before we go," I said, "there is one last thing I want to do."

"Such as what?"

"The map. I want to memorize the main features."

"An exercise in total futility."

It was an exercise in total futility to argue with her. I borrowed her eyes and studied the map once more. I developed a fair recall for the main boulevards, cross-streets, intersections, and descender shafts. There appeared to be about a dozen levels. Everything seemed to bottom out at about the twelfth or thirteenth level, almost as though some geologic feature precluded going any deeper.

"I'm ready now," I said. "Let's find a place to hide these two bodies and then we can leave." I stepped outside and walked over to the nearest door. It opened into a smallish room, full of boxes on shelves stacked to the ceiling and on the floor. Virgil sneezed. It was a dusty place. I folded back the lid of one of the boxes. It was full of files and papers. Good enough. I returned to the guard chamber, pulled the two bodies outside and into the room, and there I stacked boxes around and over them. They would eventually be found, of course, along with the two in the corridor and the two at the outer gate. But none of them would be able to tell their discoverers who had invaded their city, or why. The police would not know whom to look for, nor our purpose here.

I went back to the nearest floater and tried its door. It was locked. I didn't bother trying to break in. Like my own, the steering column was probably locked, and

even if I could hot-wire it, I wouldn't be able to steer it.
Well, never mind.

We set out on foot and eventually left the floaters
behind us.

As I looked down the streetway, I was awed and
excited. My eyes at that moment might have been
almost as big as those of an undergrounder. To think
that this great city had been here for three thousand
years, and its very existence, until recently, was
considered a myth. And here I was, actually inside,
walking its streets as though I owned the place.

The streetway soon intersected a respectably wide
avenue, lined with tall, treelike growths, and rows of
strange, dense shrubs. I hid behind a row of shrubbery
while Virgil wriggled under it, thrust her head through,
and looked carefully up and down the avenue. A
floater passed slowly, and far down the way another
was approaching. It slowed at an intersection, then
turned and disappeared. That was all. How could this
be? Where was everybody?

And then I understood. Like our own people far
above, the dwellers of Dis had adapted to a rhythm of
day and night. I had entered the grotto at dawn of my
own time, but down here it was still night. Naturally
the streets were nearly empty.

I had Virgil look up and down the street. As far as
she could see, it was completely lined with these strange
trees and shrubs. Oddly gnarled vines crawled up the
sides of the houses, and the areas in front of the houses
were planted with some sort of turflike growth. None
of this was anything like our green things in the upper
world. In fact, looking at all this through Virgil's eyes,
it seemed more of a drab grayish white, devoid of
chlorophyll. The treelike things seemed to consist of
fronds emerging from the top of a scaly trunk. The
shrubs were mostly enlarged multistemmed miniature
trees. The "grass" consisted of countless tiny,

mushroom-shaped petals. I assumed that, starting with mushrooms, toadstools, and other mycelia, they had developed a number of genetic variations for a number of different roles: some for esthetic reasons, but most to serve two very essential purposes. The first was oxygen. I was certain that these plants had some sort of "photosynthetic" cycle, based on the mysterious source of energy indicated on the abbot's map. Like plants topside, they absorbed water vapor and carbon dioxide, made starch, and gave off oxygen. Secondly, specialized mushroomlike varieties were certain to be food sources, not only for the people here, but also for their meat-source animals. Somewhere down here they had acres of cultivated crops, pastures, barns, and farm animals.

Not that it made me feel more at home. The place was still very strange indeed.

As I peered out into the dim light, I noticed winged, bird-sized creatures flitting about. I identified them tentatively as some sort of bat. And how could it be otherwise? No song birds would be here: only these mysterious creatures of the night.

"Somewhere around here," I flashed to Virgil, "is a descender. We have to go down two more levels."

The descender turned out to be an enormous spiral staircase. The great size puzzled me for a moment. Why so wide and high? Just then, as though in answer, a floater whirled around the bend of the stairwell and passed over our heads without a backward glance. We did not have time to cringe against the wall. The shaft was big because it had to accommodate vehicles as well as people.

Virgil turned to watch it disappear around the turn of the stairway.

Extraordinary, I thought. They must have seen us. And yet the hand on the steering wheel of the floater had not boggled an iota. Was it common practice for dire wolves to roam the streets of this Hades? Hardly.

But there was a simpler explanation. The driver had not reacted to Virgil because his fleeting glimpse of her had told his eyes: Man and Dog. She was a simple optical illusion.

I smiled and put my hand on her head. "Virgil, I hereby dub thee, Dog."

"And may you roast here in Hell."

We reached the second level without further incident.

This level was in the suburbs of the city. We peeked warily around the corner of the great entrance way. I saw nothing in motion. This was an area of sheds, warehouses, and light industry.

Virgil sniffed. "Some kind of food-processing plant a block or two up the road. I am hungry."

"Forget it. We both had a good meal before we hit the water."

"That was two hours ago."

"We won't die of starvation."

"You may be right."

I saw what she meant. A mysterious beam of light was moving slowly up the avenue. It was the first deliberate and continuing illumination I had seen here. To the undergrounders it must have been as glaring as a searchlight in the world above.

I studied it through Virgil's eyes. The beam came from a floater. The little ship hovered a few feet above the street, and it was moving slowly toward us, sweeping the doorways of the buildings one by one.

15. BEATRA

VIRGIL SHRANK BACK against my leg. I felt her coarse
pelt trembling, and I sensed, rather than heard, a deep
rumble in her throat.

"Police," I said. My mind message was clear and
terse.

She was totally suspicious, and justly so. "Are they
looking for us?"

"I don't know. It may be simply routine. They may
do this for all streets, perhaps even two or three times a
night. I think if they were looking for us, there would
be a dozen ships, crawling all over the place." I inhaled
deeply, then slowly let the air out of my lungs. But even
as I was replying, my heart was pounding away.
Routine or not, the situation was rapidly deteriorating.
In a matter of seconds that spotlight would sweep
slowly up and over us, then it would jerk back to us,
there to impale us with its luminous shaft. And
then...? We couldn't stay here. We both knew this.
Furthermore we had to get on to Beatra, and quickly.
Almost in the same instant we would have to deal with

this floater and be on our way. Plans, ideas, desperate schemes were forming, bubbling up, collapsing. But one kept coming back. It was so insane that it just might work.

My thought rang out to Virgil like clanging steel. "We are going to take that floater."

I thought she would immediately tell me I was crazy. But she was a female, and full of surprises. "What do you want me to do?" she asked. Her flank ceased to vibrate. Now that the moment for action had arrived, she had relaxed again.

"I am going to do a thing that will cause the floater to pull up. After it stops, one of the guards will get out and run around behind the warehouse at our rear. As soon as he goes around the corner, start after him. Kill him."

"He has a gun."

"And you, my dear, have sharp, beautiful teeth. Now, stop arguing and let me concentrate for a moment."

I looked about with her eyes. I found what I expected. There was plenty of dust and dirt in this area. It had been settling here for perhaps hundreds of years, and the place was rarely if ever cleaned.

As the floater slowly approached, I formed a spinning column from the dust on the grounds on the opposite side of the street. Virgil's ears perked up, and she watched curiously. I built the thing up until it was roughly the shape and size of a man. Then I made it lean forward a little, and I moved it rapidly across the head beam of the oncoming police vessel, toward the place where Virgil and I were hiding at the streetside. It became a fugitive, running, fleeing from the police. It was so lifelike it amazed even me.

The floater stopped instantly.

The fugitive was now across the street, and he vanished behind the building to our rear.

A guard dropped from the vessel and hit the street running toward us.

It was working. The scheme was unfolding as predictably as some well-known mummer's play at our theatre back home.

Virgil began to tremble again.

I watched the guard with her eyes as he passed us and followed the dust-phantom behind the building. In this he was not greatly different from most of us, who also pursue phantoms, and if sometimes we overtake them, likewise find them to be but dust. At least he would be spared this ultimate disillusionment.

"Take him," I said.

She flashed away silently. I listened intently, but I could not hear even the impact of her pads on the ground. The unfortunate quarry would never know what hit him. How could I so quickly and readily destroy this man whom I had never known, and who had never done me personal harm? The answer was simple. He stood across the path to my darling. He and the others, already dead, and those who might yet join him in the dark mysteries before the day was done, were obstacles to rescuing Beatra.

I let my sight vanish with Virgil, because I knew what would happen next, and I knew I would be busy with my next problem.

When the second guard saw the savage shape bound around the corner after his cohort, he immediately jumped from the floater and started running toward us. I heard and sensed this, rather than saw it.

And now I would have to take a real chance. In order to be sure of killing this man with an electropistol I needed light. If I fired one shot, that would give me enough light for a second shot, but if I missed him then, he would be around the corner, and the third shot would be his, and I would be dead, and *he* would have the right to declare who pursued phantoms. No, that way was too risky. But there were other light sources.

As he passed me, I formed a tiny luminous air globe six feet over my head, and behind me. It was a little thing, but to him it must have been a sunburst. He whirled instantly, blinded, and threw an arm over his eyes. I fired. By the globe-light I saw blood gush from a great round hole that suddenly appeared in his throat. His arm fell away, then he put a hand to the flood in his jugular. Then his knees buckled, and he dropped.

At that moment Virgil trotted around the corner, licking blood from her chops. "Did you take care of yours?" I asked. She tossed her muzzle. So stupid a question was totally beneath her contempt. I smiled grimly, collapsed the light point, and took over her eyes. "Look toward the building again," I said, "while I drag this one around the corner."

So now I—we—had killed eight men. Did I feel remorse? Regrets? Quite the contrary. For one of them had told me where Beatra was being held, and two had brought me their floater, almost as if I had ordered it up for hire. Besides which they had clothed me and provided me with weapons. I felt grateful!

After I disposed of the corpse, I returned to the floater. "Let's see if we can make this thing work." The door was still open, and the motor was still running. It leaned very slightly as we got in, then the gyros righted it. Virgil looked it over quickly. It had two seats, a radio box, restraint bars in the back to hold prisoners, weapon racks, fire extinguisher, and a few other things I could not immediately identify. But otherwise it was very like my own personal floater which my grandfather had found buried in debris-shale near New Bollamer, and which we had restored together in his shops. It probably operated on the antigravity principle, the same as mine. (But what the antigravity principle is, and how it works, I don't know, and shall never understand.)

Everything was falling into place. And there was an

extra piece of luck. Just before the floater had stopped, it had shone its beam on the door of the fatal warehouse, and I had read the sign:

EMIGRATION
EMERGENCY FUEL OIL

Oil? The very fact that the stuff existed here invited conjecture and speculation. (How did they get it? Did they drill even deeper into the earth's crust and pump it up from pools, as the ancients are said to have done? Did they synthesize it? If so, how, and from what? What use did a nuclear-powered civilization have for fuel oil? And finally, what was this "Emigration"?) But it was pointless and time-wasting even to think about it.

I left the machine and walked over to the building. It was locked, of course. I kicked the door in. Musty clouds of dust swirled out of the darkness. I coughed. Virgil sneezed, then stepped gingerly inside, and I took her eyes. The oil was in ceramic containers stacked in large wooden crates. Some sort of vegetable fiber was packed in between the jars, apparently to minimize breakage. I gathered up an armful of the shredded fibers and a couple of the clay urns. I tossed the fiber packing all around the floor of the floater, then I put the jars behind the driver's seat.

Virgil sniffed dubiously. "I hope you know what you're doing."

I closed the floater door. "Be quiet. I have to experiment a moment with the controls." Everything checked. Forward and reverse were governed by a floor pedal, the same as on my own craft back home. Right and left turns were controlled by a steering wheel, and descent and ascent by moving the steering column forward or back. The only real difference seemed to be the rate of ascent. That was understandable. Too swift a climb would crash the thing into the street ceiling. There were a couple of unfamiliar viewing screens. They gave views of the surfaces of the street and ceiling, below and overhead. These extra screens would be useful, especially to me, the unskilled intruder.

I turned the ship around, and we started off slowly down the street.

"Where now?" asked Virgil.

"To the next descender. There ought to be one about a mile down the road." I was glad now that I had taken the trouble in the guardhouse to memorize that map. It now glowed and scintillated in my mind. To the descender. Down another five levels. Then forward down a broad avenue, half a mile to a cluster of walled buildings. And somewhere, in there, was my beloved. But not for long. *We were coming!*

The street was empty. We reached the descender shaft without incident.

I now understood a further purpose of the two additional viewing screens in the front panel. Out in the street they had shown simply the surfaces of the street and the street ceiling. In the street, I had little need of them. There, all I had really needed were front and rear views. But now I had to descend, and I had to know what was below as well as what was above the ship. The screens provided this information quite adequately. Far below, there did indeed appear to be one dim red light slowly rising. Since my present craft had three tiny red lights in a triangle, this meant to me that the ascending floater was not a police ship. That was fine with me. I watched it continue to ascend for a few seconds. If I stayed where I was, it would crash into the bottom of my ship. I must be in the wrong lane. I moved over into the left-hand area of the great shaft and began a cautious descent.

"Sit up here in front with me," I commanded the huntress. "I hereby promote you to police dog. Just look alert; a little grim, perhaps."

She sneered.

We dropped past the rising ship fairly quickly. It had one occupant. He looked at us curiously, then held up his hand in greeting. Was the dead driver of this machine supposed to know him? I doubted it. I held my hand up in brief, languid acknowledgment, and then he was above us. The next moment I picked up the green lights of the bottom of his ship in my front panel. And then he was gone altogether. Apparently he had turned off on the next side street. But I couldn't worry about him. If he had radioed the central police about a suspicious patrol ship, there was absolutely nothing I could do about it. I had to proceed on the assumption that my presence here was still unsuspected.

I dropped the ship another four levels, to the seventh, then moved out into what must have been the widest, most spacious boulevard in the entire city. It was lined on either side by great and strange trees, and bordering them were parks containing shrubs, trees, statuary, and fountains.

All of this came to a dead end half a mile down the avenue. For here rose the great flickering facade of what had to be their vaunted White House. A patrol of guardsmen passed briskly in front of this great building. With Virgil's eyes, this was the only movement that I could detect. The place was protected by a stone wall, head-high, and above this an immense grill of one-inch bars stretched from the wall to the boulevard ceiling. As I had anticipated, there was indeed a gate for the entrance of floaters. The gate was another iron grid, much like the one I had encountered in the grotto, except that this one was considerably larger. A few feet away from the gate was a doorway. Even as I watched, a guard walked casually out of the doorway and looked up and down the broad walkway in front of the building. My mind reached out for his. The contact wisps slid along the crevices of his occipital area, probing, searching.

This was the place! This man had been on duty at this very gate when the kidnap party had returned with her that fateful night. And she was still here!

The guard re-entered the post, and the little door closed behind him.

I was beginning to tremble. Virgil looked up at me and whined.

And now my mind reached behind the forbidding walls. There were many people inside, moving about on the inner court. How could that be? It was night here. The people should be home in their beds. In this White House, however, something special seemed to be going on. I seized upon one mind at random for a closer study. The man was evidently another guard, one of a small group. He and his group were standing beside a floater, at the entrance port. He seemed to be waiting for something...for someone...or perhaps for an event. The thought images were coming in strongly...the White House...the doors opening... here they come...I see her...

Her?

I cast my mind net in the direction I thought the guard was looking. I caught a group...of men...and now a woman. But it wasn't Beatra. And then I had it. If Beatra were being brought out of the White House, she would of course be accompanied by one or more women guards. It was a female guard whose mind I had touched. But why were they bringing my darling out? I couldn't imagine. Nor did I care. It was a piece of incredible good fortune. This way, I wouldn't have to break in and make a building-to-building search, while *they* were searching for *me*.

I was back again, this time touching one mind after another. Male, female, sometimes repeating. They were now all very close to the invisible ship.

And then my insides seemed to turn upside down. *Beatra!* I had found her!

Did she know I was here? That my mind was

touching hers? "Beatra! Beatra!" I called to her mind. "I am here! I have come for you! Stay! Stay!" Although I could not see her, I knew that she was looking wildly about her, and that she had heard my mental voice. They began to drag her forcibly.

Where were they taking her? Back inside? There was no reason to do that. But they didn't seem to be heading for the exit grid, either. With desperate urgency I searched for the mind of the chief guard, or the pilot, a matron, anyone who knew the ship's destination. I found wisps of information here and there. Something about a further descent, to a gloomy, forbidding place. A maximum security prison of some type.

The immediate and rather horrid problem was, they were not coming out on the boulevard. There seemed to be some sort of floater-port located *within* the White House grounds, a great private shaft that went up and down to other levels. I had found her, but now I was about to lose her again—this time perhaps indefinitely.

She must not get on that ship. I had to do something, and quickly. Fortunately, I came prepared. I swung my little craft around and pointed its nose at the great gate. I turned back into the floater, seized the two jars, and shattered them against the bed of strawlike material that I had spread behind the seats. Next, I fired a shot with my electropistol into the oil-drenched straw. It began to burn.

"Get out," I commanded Virgil. She obeyed with alacrity, for she greatly feared the growing flames. I grabbed a rifle from the racks, jumped out on my side of the ship, then reached through the open door and laid the rifle across the accelerator pedal. The little ship leaped forward.

Events now followed as though I had written a play-drama for them. The blazing ship struck the big grill-gate dead center, and dropped, a red-tongued inferno. The patrol came stumbling back up the walkway, blind, holding their hands over their eyes. Three men groped their way through the guard doorway, likewise shielding their eyes. I rather suspected they might be permanently blinded. They were ill prepared to deal with such a catastrophe. One man went back in and emerged with some sort of smallish fire extinguisher. Whether he ever used it, I will never know, because, in the red glare I had seen flickering shapes through the iron gate, and the big floater, buoyant at the dock. I burst through the guard doorway, with Virgil close behind, and dashed for the floater. Two women were dragging a third woman across the entrance board that stuck out, tonguelike, under the ship door. Before they disappeared into the vessel I caught a glimpse of a face. It turned back, searching, and contorted by its own anguish and by the fantasies of the flames. Oh beloved, what have they done to you! The funeral scars on my chest began to pulse and drum.

Through the acrid, drifting smoke and the flames of the burning floater, I saw that the great metal plates of the White House exit shaft were fully open, above and below, and Beatra's ship was now moving slowly out into the gaping void.

Incredibly, the ship door was still open, and just below it, the entrance tongue-board was still extended. The tongue-board jutted out about two feet from the shipside.

"Come!" I signaled Virgil. I ran. I knocked people down. I leaped across the gap to the tongue-board. The wolf was just behind me.

Several things happened. I had already noted two figures just beyond the doorway. I saw their faces, and I recognized both. One was the man they called the President.

The other was Beatra.

He was pulling her aside and simultaneously pushing a lever by the doorside.

All of this was happening while Virgil and I were in midair.

The door slammed shut in my face. I was frozen there, balanced precariously on the little step with Virgil, looking into the ship through a glass porthole, and they were in the corridor looking back at me, in the wavering red light of the flames behind me, believing and unbelieving. I looked at them both, but I saw only her. Her hair was in tangles. Her face was thin and drawn, her eyes were sunken and shadowed. They had interrogated her, and they had done terrible things. But I looked at her and beheld only beauty.

"Jerrie!" shrieked Beatra. I could hear it through the ship walls. She broke away and began to beat on the door with her fists. We looked at each other through that cruel glass for seconds.

The President came up behind her. For an instant his pale features adjoined hers in a horrid cameo. His lips (which looked as though they had been added to his mouth by sardonic afterthought) parted, and his teeth gave up a wolfish grin in the firelight. He had grasped the total situation very quickly. He understood who I was. And then he threw his head back, laughed, and pulled a lever by the entranceway.

The little tongue-board scraped into the side of the ship.

We hung there for a fraction of a second. Virgil began to moan.

At first the fall was slow, almost leisurely. I had time to sense the chill, indignant air that we were disturbing. I remember looking up at the tiny green running lights of the bottom of Beatra's ship, and that they were turning in slow tight circles. And then we were plummeting down, down, into blackness.

16. THE RIVER

I THOUGHT: what a moronic way to die. Crushed on the hard limestone floor of this monstrous shaft. I had been so close, and now it had all come to this.

Instinctively I brought my knees up under my chin, in the fetal position. I would die as I had been born, under protest. I remember doing this, and taking a deep sigh, perhaps in regret that I had failed Beatra, perhaps in self-pity for my untimely end. And then . . . I struck something . . . with an enormous *plack*. I was under water . . . *way* under. And spluttering, and gasping, and clawing upward, and strangling. There was something down there with me. Virgil, of course. I got under her and pushed her upward with me through the dark water. After an age we broke the surface. She was unconscious. Perhaps even dead. I tried without success to make mental contact. I had lost one boot; I kicked off the other. I held Virgil's head up while I treaded water and looked about.

Nothing. But at least I was no longer the total fatalistic failure that I had been seconds past, in midfall. I was alive again. Life was good, and I knew with certainty that I would find Beatra and bring her out again. Time had passed, and my precious twenty-four hours was fading, but the prophecies were still with me. I could do it.

Yet... I had to think about what they intended to do with her now. Where were they taking her? What were they going to do to her? I shivered.

Meanwhile, I tried to look about, while I held Virgil's head clear of the water. I squinted, wiped the water out of my eyes with my free hand, and peered out again.

Total darkness everywhere.

I looked up. Nothing there, either. Just more cold, wet blackness. The green lights of Beatra's ship had disappeared. Perhaps it had gone off into one of the intersecting corridors far above me. But how far above, and to what distance, I had no way of knowing. Perhaps the interrogation was over. Perhaps they were through with her, and they were now taking her for an indefinite stay in a close-security prison. Perhaps... But I had to stop this. At the moment I could do nothing for her, and there were very immediate things I had to face here.

They knew now that they could be invaded. They knew I had done it. They knew why I had come, and they must soon discover how I had got as far as I had. The burning floater would be quickly identified; its patrol route would be carefully retraced. The bodies would be found. The guardpost would next be checked, and more bodies would be found. And finally they would send a full platoon up the tunnel to the great grotto, and they would then know my exact path, from start to finish.

And now the big question. Would they assume that I had been killed in my long, breathtaking fall, or would they come looking for me? There was no way to know for sure. They might follow us down, if only to confirm that there was no trace of us, and that therefore we could be presumed dead.

All of this passed through my mind in a flash. And it added up to this: we had to get out of here.

I was calm enough now to make a vortectic concentration. I lay on my back, with one arm under Virgil, and formed a large, luminous sphere, some forty feet overhead. It seemed to be surrounded by two or three soft iridescent rings, a phenomenon caused, I thought, by the water vapor that saturated the air. As my eyes grew accustomed to the light I studied my furry friend. Dark wavelets lapped about the white fur at her neckline. Her eyes were glazed and half-shut. She was still unconscious, but she was breathing. She probably had a lot of water in her lungs. I would have to find some kind of flat surface to stretch her out and empty her lungs. I looked up and around. Light reflected back at us from a glistening, stalactite-festooned ceiling of a vast underground cavern. Off slightly to one side, a great hole in the ceiling marked the entranceway of the shaft through which we had fallen.

The pillars arising from the riverbed puzzled me at first. All, or nearly all, of them were paired. Each stalactite that hung from the ceiling was matched by a stalagmite that rose up beneath it. Some of the pairs were fused into one great pillar, which stood there as though given the task of supporting the ceiling. This much offered no mystery. I knew that stalactites and stalagmites were formed by water dripping from the ceiling over thousands of years. The origin of the stalactites hanging from the roof was easy to perceive. That of the stalagmites was not immediately evident; for as the water dripped into the river, it would not be possible to build up a corresponding column on the river bottom, because the drippings would simply be swept away. But in considering this, I got an insight into the majestic workings of time. The

cavern had been formed first, probably by being
washed out by water, millennia ago. Then the waters
receded, and the cavern bottoms were left to dry. Then
the stalactites and stalagmites began slowly to form,
until they reached very nearly their present size. And
then, through some huge convulsion of the earth's
crust, perhaps only two or three millennia ago, the
waters returned. And now man and wolf rode as chips
on the waters of geologic time.

But the most astonishing thing was this: the
shaftway in the ceiling was very definitely moving, and
along with it, the adjacent cluster of stalactites that
hung from the great cavern roof. That was quite
impossible, of course, and the solution hit me soon
enough, in a very literal sense. For we bumped against
a large rock pinnacle thrusting up from the water.
We—were moving.

We were in some sort of broad subterranean river.

The Returner had mentioned a river. The Brothers
had even given it a name: the mythical Lethe. Well, it
was no myth. It was real, and it was bad, because it was
taking us farther from Beatra by the second.

Where did the river end? It was clearly below sea
level. It couldn't empty into the sea. Was there some
great subterranean ocean here that never filled? I asked
the questions, but I found that I did not really want to
know the answers. I wanted *not* to understand, but I
had to understand. I forced myself to accept this dread
knowledge. And now it was coming to me. This was the
underground river by which the Returner had escaped,
threading his way through the stone pillars in a stolen
floater. This living fluid flowed down, down, to the
molten vitals of the earth, there to suffer its great
transformation. For it had to return again to the
surface, this time as red-hot steam.

We were headed for the Spume.

I had a momentary vision of its titanic, searing

power. We would go up that holocaust column not as corpses, but as bits and pieces of overcooked flesh and shattered bone, to be strewn helterskelter over miles of drear landscape. And now I thought back to the night I had spent in the dead tree near the Spume, and how I had shoved a collection of bones from the branch crotch at my back, and how I had wondered how it had gotten there. Well, now I knew. Would I likewise conclude as buzzard bait, miles and hours away?

Despite the chill water, I found that I was perspiring profusely. We had to get out, immediately!

I swept the blackness from side to side with the light-ball, searching for a shore, a place to climb out and try to revive my friend. I saw only a brooding forest of stone pillars in front of me, to either side, and behind me. I sensed invisible backwaters of crystal lakes, icy pools, tributary streams. All very fine. But how to get out? How to get some solid ground under us? To start, there had to be a shore. Two shores, in fact. One on either side of the river. Which was closer?

I struck out for the nearest stalagmite and let the current hold us against its cold, wet side for a little while. I brought the light near and examined the rock carefully. It tapered upward, smooth as ice, except for intermittent vertical striations, and it was almost as cold as ice. It seemed to terminate in a point. It offered nothing.

As I paused there, treading water in frustration, I began to notice...the *vibrations*. Something was happening to the water. It was trembling. Strange ripples appeared on the surface, and here and there tiny white-crested wave tops appeared. I felt the stone pillar shaking. My heart seemed to rise to my throat and to stick there, pounding. Then the sounds came. At first it was a low, crackling moan. Then, very quickly, it became a continuous booming groan, and it grew louder and louder. I could not localize it. It seemed to be coming from everywhere at once.

Another temblor? A full-sized quake? I looked about in alarm.

I lofted the light sphere high overhead and swept the ceiling area immediately above us. The ball seemed to jiggle in sympathy with my own mental shudders.

There was a great limestone stalactite pointing down at our pillar. It seemed blurred. I shook my head quickly and looked again. It still seemed somehow out of focus. And then I knew why. It, too, was shuddering. As was every stalactite and stalagmite in the river. Each was vibrating cumbrously at its own subsonic frequency.

And at that moment there was a crack like a thousand thunderbolts, and I watched with total horror as the great stone dagger dropped toward us.

I was frozen in fear and dismay. And I might as well have been, because there was absolutely nothing I could do.

The stony point of the giant monolith crashed squarely into the top of its lower counterpart, hung there, still upright, massively casual, as though it intended to maintain that delicate, impossible balance forever, then began to fall lazily, *away* from us. The air around it began to shriek as it arced downward, slowly and gracefully at first, then faster, and finally irresistibly. It crashed into the water on the other side of our sheltering pillar, and there followed a flood of waves and spray, noisy and prolonged. But the water finally quieted, and it was over. Still holding Virgil, I paddled around to the fallen colossus. It took me a moment to make a new light-ball (the first one having collapsed during the excitement). The great pillar had broken in two and was lying on its side, with a considerable part of its surface out of the water. Judging from its apparent diameter and its angle of rest, I estimated the water depth here to be twelve to fifteen feet. The fallen mass was wet and slippery, but now its striations were nearly horizontal rather than vertical, and actually offered hand holds of a sort. By dint of much slipping and sliding I got Virgil up on top of it. I detected a strong heartbeat as I pulled her from the water. She was still very much alive. There should be some way to bring her around.

I stretched her out on her belly and began to press rhythmically on her back and sides. Water, amid froth and bubbles, gushed out of her muzzle and nostrils for the first couple of strokes. I kept it up. Soon the wheezings and gurglings began. The noise from her lungs quickly reached some sort of maximum, then gradually faded as the minutes passed. I called out to her from time to time, both mentally and orally. "Virgil! Wake up, wake up!"

Finally she groaned, opened her eyes, and sneezed. I stepped back and waited.

She got up groggily, looked around, and began to shake the water out of her coat. Her tail was last, and it sent a fine spray directly in my face. This, I knew, was deliberate. I sighed. Completely ignoring me, she began a slow full turn on the fallen rock, sniffing the air and turning her head this way and that. Her ears were pricked to a full alert.

I thought she was going to berate me, tell me how stupid I had been. I know she felt that way, and I was inclined to agree with her. But she merely said, "Do we have to have that silly light?"

"Not if it bothers you."

"It bothers me."

I shrugged my shoulders and collapsed the light. It didn't really matter for the time being. Also, I sensed that she was leading up to something important, and she wanted to minimize extraneous distractions.

With the light gone, the great cavern was totally dark, and almost as still. At first I was partially blinded by the imaginary afterglow of the light sphere. This passed. Finally I could see nothing, and I could hear nothing save the faint flow of the water past our rock.

She flashed a mental question, deceptively casual and matter-of-fact. "Can you hear it?"

And now I truly did feel stupid. I strained my ears. It was worse than useless. I could no longer detect even the water lapping around our precarious roost. "Hear *what*?" I demanded.

"The waterfall."

My spine tingled, and then I stiffened. The long and tortured drop of the river to the molten magma would of course start with a waterfall. Oh, let this not be! No shore in sight. Did Lethe, the river of forgetfulness, which now held us firm in its watery grasp, propose to dash us to death before expelling us up the Spume? This was death too close! It was not fair! I had to deny the whole thing. "No," I said, "I don't hear a waterfall."

"It's there. Relax. Stop making so much noise. Take your time, and listen again."

I faced downstream, held my breath, and listened. And waited. And now at long last I *could* hear something. A faint, almost subaudible moaning. My heart sank, and I wanted to moan with it. "Yes," I said glumly, "I hear it."

"If we try to swim out of here, we will be swept over the fall."

There was no point in explaining the Spume to her. The falls were bad enough. I simply said: "We absolutely have to get out, and the only way is to swim. Which shore," I demanded, "is closer?"

"We'll both be killed."

"Would you prefer to die of starvation?"

"There're fish in this river. Maybe I can catch some."

"Sure. Use your tail as bait."

"You don't have to be crude."

"Sorry. Well, goodbye, Virgil."

She looked up in alarm and accusation. "You'd leave without me?"

"Yes."

"Moosedung!" she flashed bitterly. "Well, wait just a minute." She gave a short yip, then listened intently. She tossed her head. "The closer shore is over there."

It was obviously an intuitive judgment, made merely on the basis of echoes. But I trusted it.

"How far?"

"A hundred yards."

I sucked in my breath. Quite a distance. There was indeed considerable risk. But on the other hand, it was useless, even foolish, to remain. Aside from the fact that it was completely futile to sit forever on this lifeless rock, there were other, intangible dangers. For example, a bevy of floaters might be dropping down the shaft behind us at this very moment.

I was thinking aloud, not only to help me make a decision, but also to keep Virgil informed as to the various factors I was taking into consideration.

"There is," she observed dryly, "a still further, very important consideration."

"What is that?"

"Form your light again. Over there." She pointed with her muzzle.

I quickly made a glow-sphere, high in the air in the general direction she indicated. And by its light I saw the great arching neck, loathsome white eyes above the barrel-sized jaws, the glistening rows of teeth. Some sort of water dragon was sweeping down on us. Foam and spray were bursting ahead of its chest, like the bow-wave on a ship. Its questing head was poised a good dozen feet above the water. The light didn't bother it at all. It was very likely totally blind, and located its prey by sound and scent. Very likely this devil fed on smaller creatures, and these on still smaller. There must be a full chain of river life, supported by garbage and human waste dumped into Lethe by the people of Dis. Just as the falls would take our lives before we reached the Spume, so would this creature cheat the falls. Death had stolen a second march on us.

My hand jerked to first one holster, then the other. I had lost both electropistols.

And now, as on certain previous occasions of great danger, the duration of time (that flux so mysterious, yet so inexorable) suddenly slowed. Motion very nearly ceased. The horrid head stayed its downward swoop. A gush of foamy saliva hung suspended from the monster's chin.

I knew, of course, that time moves on at its own steady pace forever. It does not languish upon the whim or pleasure of any mortal. I knew that it was my own sensibilities that had so remarkably accelerated in a reflex attempt to save my life. And indeed, I had already firmly resolved not to vanish down the cavern-throat of this slimy devil.

I forced my mind into a fantastic effort of will. The light sphere shrank. It was now so hot that it turned blue, and so brilliant that I could not bear to look at it directly. I was astonished. I had never made a heat-ball before. But I wasted no time in admiring the product of this great effort! I drove it straight into that gaping muzzle, into the pea-sized brain, and out the other side. There was the instant stench of seared flesh, followed by a horrid, prolonged scream. The great neck began to thresh from side to side. It flailed at our fallen stalactite perch a couple of times. Even in the mindless act of dying it was still dangerous. Once the great body crashed back into the water so hard that the waves swamped us, and the foam struck the ceiling and poured back on us in torrents. Virgil and I slid off the rock and cowered in the water on the other side from the creature. The threshing continued for several minutes, then faded away. The great body was gone. It had either sunk beneath the water or had floated away.

I let the heat-point expand to a light-ball, and looked about us. All seemed quiet.

"Come on," I said, and struck out for the nearer shore. Virgil followed without a word. She knew what I was thinking: did this monster have a mate? Are there still others out there? I was quite content to leave the question hanging unanswered. And the best way to do that was to get out as quickly as possible.

Swimming crosscurrent always presents a curious illusion. Actually, you move in two directions. You move downstream right along with the current, while at the same time you are trying to swim at right angles to it. The resultant vector is a diagonal, but you don't realize this except with reference to fixed points on the streambed or on the shore. Well, we couldn't see the shore, but we could see any number of stalagmites. And these seemed to be sweeping upstream at an ever increasing velocity.

The sound of the falls was now becoming very loud—a full, droning boom. We had made progress, but it was not possible to say how much. Perhaps we were halfway to the shore. I let the light-ball hover near an emergent column, and I signaled to Virgil to join me there in a moment's rest, while we let the current push us against the side of the rock. The river was now flowing very fast. Here and there were signs of turbulence and white water. The moan of the falls drowned out everything. My anxiety seemed to increase with the din of the falls, making it very difficult for me to concentrate.

Virgil was glum but stoical. She had already decided that we were not going to make it. She had paddled valiantly behind and beside me, but with foreknowledge of how it would end. She was still fighting, but more out of a feeling of bitter pride than in any conviction of ultimate success.

"Here we go," I said. I dove off into the current once more. She followed me. Not with confidence, but out of a dearth of alternates. The river tumbled me over once before I readjusted to it. I grabbed a handful of fur at one point and pulled Virgil around to my upstream side. I did not want her to get separated from me. We went through a rapid before we ever knew it was coming, and we both went under for a few seconds. Then we were up again, and battling. To my surprise, the light-ball was still there when we resurfaced.

It revealed the shore—a bare twenty yards away. I shouted in great elation, and we struck out for it.

And then my heart sank.

The shore—if such it could be called—was a sheer cliff of limestone, water polished and glass smooth. There was no horizontal edge where we might crawl out. I raised the light-ball higher as we struggled toward this illusory salvation. Now I could see that there was indeed a ledge, some ten or twelve feet above the water, carved out, perhaps, when the river level was higher. Only ten feet, but way over our heads. It might as well have been a mile high.

If Virgil hadn't been there, I think I would have burst into tears. I might even have thought about ceasing this long and idiotic struggle, given myself up to the clamoring water, and looked to rejoining Beatra in death. But I wasn't given the opportunity to explore these dark, seductive thoughts. The paradox was lost on me at the moment, but actually we were saved by another disaster.

Virgil, still swimming grimly beside me, signaled succinctly: "Another . . . *thing* . . . is coming. Its mate, I think."

Defeat and fatigue were instantly tossed aside. I looked back, strangely unalarmed, as though my attention might have been invited to a curious geological formation, or to a larger than usual stone pillar. The reason for my lack of fear was that I was too tired to react properly. Exhaustion smothers fright.

The thing was perhaps a hundred yards upstream. I watched with interest the approach of the great lizard neck, the enormous muscles rippling under the wet, black skin in a sort of lethal beauty. The jaws now opened wide in glittering anticipation. He—or she— swept gracefully down at us, as though there were no problem with the current at all.

There was one more stalagmite between us and the cliff shore. I motioned to Virgil to head for it. We reached the haven of the pillar and immediately I turned to face the demon. I condensed the light sphere to an acorn-sized heat-ball. I shouted my defiance with all the strength of my lungs and I crashed the ball into the base of the creature's skull from the rear. The searing ball interrupted its dazzling arc but briefly as it passed through the brain and then zipped like a fiery tongue through the open jaws, after which it struck the pillar not far over my head and rebounded into the air, where it hung, radiant, blue-hot, and vengeful, as though searching for other beasts to slay.

By that warlike glow we watched the passing of this second behemoth. The colossal neck dropped into the water, and there the current caught it. The creature tumbled over and over, and was swept away in seconds. Did it scream? Did it convulse in an incomprehending death agony? There was no way to know. All sound and all suffering yielded to the far greater torture and howls of the great river as it leapt toward the engulfing falls.

And now I looked overhead where the heat-ball had struck our stalagmite. There seemed to be a fist-sized hole there. Ah! I had an immediate inspiration. A hole? But not *just* a hole. Rather, a way out. Salvation. Virgil watched me curiously as I tossed a handful of water at the hole. It sizzled, probably for two reasons. Firstly, it was still very hot. Secondly, the heat of the ball had converted some of the limestone into quicklime, which, when slaked with water, had given off considerable heat.

Farewell, falls! Farewell, Spume! Beatra, we are coming!

I looked over at the shore wall, estimated where we would strike it after we crossed the remaining yards of torrent, and then I added another couple of yards downstream to be on the safe side. Next I commanded the little ball of blue heat to strike the cliff wall where I expected to make contact, one foot above the water line, then again, one foot higher, and then again and again, all the way up to the lip of the ledge. Afterward, I let the heat-ball expand into a light-ball, and I stationed it overhead. Next I formed a whirling sphere of water, and I carefully washed out each of the pockets I had made. Finally, I pulled my shoulder harness around Virgil's back and chest, and placed the terminal loop over my shoulder.

To get ready, I tried to take a few deep breaths. But the air was full of spray, and I had to spit out a mouthful. No matter. For the first time since striking the water, I felt almost cheerful. I signaled to Virgil: "We're going up the side of the wall."

"Yes."

Mercifully she didn't demand to know what I intended to do after we crawled up over the ledge. Which way led to Beatra? Downriver? Upriver? Or perhaps we were on the wrong shore? It was futile to wonder about it.

"Now!" I cried.

We struck out through the crashing water together. We reached the wall by efforts that were superhuman and superwolf. And I was glad indeed that I had provided for some leeway in placing the bottom hand holes. If I had placed them six inches farther upstream, we would have missed them, owing to the incredible strength of the current. I clung with both hands to the lowest slot a moment, panting and gasping, and spewing water out of my mouth and nostrils. Virgil was in much worse shape. The white water was pulling at her so strongly that the leather harness was stretched out taut as a steel rod. I moved up to the next grab hole. At least that got her head clear of the water. By the third hole, my shoulder was taking her full weight of seventy pounds, and it was slow going. I had to make rest stops of a couple of minutes between each set of holes. She was beginning to wheeze and gurgle. The straps had tangled across her throat and chest and were suffocating her. But I could do nothing about it. "Just a few more to go!" I signaled. She grunted. When I finally reached the top she was on the verge of blacking out; and for that matter, so was I. My arms and legs had turned to rubber.

I pulled her up onto the ledge, removed the straps, and then crawled to the rear of the ledge and lay flat, pressing against the cliff side. After a moment, she joined me.

I dissolved the light sphere. For a long time we simply lay there on the cold, wet, stone surface, panting, wet, miserable, totally exhausted, and stupefied by the thunderous crashing of the falls. From its sound, it could not be more than a dozen yards away.

These waters would continue, in the ever descending channel, crashing and screaming, to their doom at the interface of hell. But they would not carry us. We had escaped. For the time being.

My thoughts went to the Brothers, and to Father Phaedrus and his dying hour. *They* had put me underground. They had been glad to do it. Because of some impossible thing they hoped I would do to the gods-eye, hundreds of miles overhead and now totally invisible. To them, Beatra was almost irrelevant. What, exactly, did they expect of me? They seemed to think that merely getting me underground would automatically result in something cataclysmic. If only they could see me now—wet, shivering, exhausted, without the faintest idea of what to do next. I looked over at my companion. And *you* (I thought) think that *you* feel confused and unreal.

She grunted wearily. "Go ahead. Be cryptic. Who gives a damn."

So she was indifferent. I had a remedy for indifference.

I started to get up.

"Don't move!" she warned.

I caught the note of sudden danger. "More creatures?"

"Floaters!"

"How many?"

"Two—no, three."

Of course. They were looking for us. Dead or alive.

17. Colonel Aksel

As THEY CAME nearer I was able to touch the minds of
the men in the floater nearest us. One by one, but
quickly, I sorted out the six minds, two to a ship. A
colonel was in charge. He was in the front ship with an
aide.

I listened carefully to the conversation in the lead
ship.

"Did the President actually *see* the fellow?" the
colonel asked his aide dubiously.

"It was so reported, sir."

"But I understand a floater had crashed into the
gate, there was a fire, and much confusion. The
President might have been mistaken."

"That is true."

"Nevertheless, we have to look."

"Yes, sir."

They were indeed looking for me. Apparently not
Virgil; just me. Evidently Virgil had not been visible to
the President through the little window in Beatra's
ship. I think the colonel had already made up his mind

that I did not exist, or that if I ever had, I was now dead. He tossed off a remark to his pilot: "After all, we execute condemned men by dropping them down the Great Shaft. If they are not killed when they hit the water, the dinos get them soon after." And the other replied, "Or, if they escape all that, they go over the falls. There is no way out. These cliffs are completely vertical on both sides, all the way up and down the river."

Now this colonel was an interesting person. He was saying these things. He was restating death and destruction in casual, almost weary cadences, as though these were routine and indifferent things to him. But I was reading him, and I knew that this high officer hated to deal in pain, suffering, and death. He was two people: an officer to the credit of his government—yet a man subversive to the disciplined requirements of that government. A soldier—and a traitor.

The colonel was now shouting to be heard over the noise. "We have reached the falls. You can turn off the hunt-beams. Tell the others we are breaking off the search. They are to return to base. We will go on to the Vortex Chamber."

"Yes, sir."

Vortex Chamber? Did it have anything to do with my own vortectic powers? More and more interesting!

I crawled out a little and peeked out over the ledge. Upstream the two following craft had already wheeled around; their lights were fading as they moved slowly back upriver, threading and weaving through the stone pillars. As the remaining craft passed our ledge all I could see were the four faint headlights, forming broad white cylinders of light by reflecting into the mist and spray thrown up by the falls. Nothing was visible inside the floater. The internal lights were off. In a moment the headlights moved around a slight bend in the canyon, beyond the falls, and everything was dark again.

I lay there on my belly for a full five minutes, waiting to make sure they were all really gone, then I got to my feet. Virgil got up silently. I borrowed her eyes and peered upstream. The view was not too good. For one thing, her visuo-reception was limited to infrared, and the trouble with that was, everything here had almost exactly the same chill temperature. It was hard to form a three-dimensional image, or to see anything in perspective. On the other hand, if anything had been moving, it would have stood out in fair relief. However, numerous stalagmites and stalactites cut off considerable portions of the view, so I could not be absolutely sure. I wanted to wait a little longer before forming a light-ball. "Meanwhile," I said to Virgil, "let's walk along the ledge."

"Up or down?"

"Down, I think. We'll follow the ship toward the falls. There seems to be something beyond the falls, something they call the Vortex Chamber."

I had no idea what the Vortex Chamber was. Yet I was becoming more and more certain that it had a direct bearing on my vortectic powers. And certainly, in those powers lay my main hope of saving Beatra. I had a destiny with this place.

"What *is* this Vortex Chamber?" asked Virgil.

I thought of the abbot's map, and the concentric circles. And the center of the circles fixed over some fantastic energy source far underground. But what *kind* of energy source? I did not know. Not yet. So I answered her the best way I knew how—which was no answer at all: "The Chamber's where they keep the Vortex, whatever *that* is."

"You don't make any sense, and I'm hungry."

"Later. Right now, just lend me your eyes, and let's be on our way."

It was easy going for the most part. The ledge was rarely less than three feet wide, and it was always fairly level. On occasion we encountered side corridors and shafts leading into the cliff side along the path. These had evidently been dissolved out by the river or by percolating water ages ago, possibly even before the time of the ancients. But we have no reason or need to explore any of these.

A five-minute walk brought us to the edge of the falls.

Virgil shrank back against the cliff side, blinking and squinting to keep the spray out of her eyes. Momentarily I left her eyes and formed a light-ball high over the rim of the falls. We moved on down the ledge another hundred yards so that I could see the crash of the water into the canyon floor far below. The noise, the titanic volume of water, and the incredible drop, all combined to take my breath away. I grew dizzy, and my legs felt weak. With Virgil I shrank back against the cliff side. "Let's get out of here," I said shakily.

She went on ahead. Spurred by the desire to find the Vortex Chamber and also to put as much distance as possible between us and the gut-shattering falls, we made good time. Fortunately the ledge stayed wide and smooth, and there was no trouble.

We had proceeded in this fashion for about ten minutes, when Virgil signaled silently: "We are coming to something."

I stopped instantly and made the light-ball vanish. With the light gone I could of course see nothing, but it might be dangerous to keep it activated. It would announce our presence immediately. I listened, but the falls still smothered all sound as it rushed down toward its fatal rendezvous. By now the channel lay at least half a mile below us, and the river fell deeper with every step we took. Within another mile or so it would probably disappear altogether. I probed for signs of life as far as I could with the tendrils of my mind, but there was nothing. "What is it?" I said. "Can you see anything?"

"Not yet."

But I trusted her. There was something there, and not too far downstream. I screened the area mentally again. Again, nothing. "I can't sense anything downstream. What do you think it is?"

She pointed her muzzle downriver and sniffed the air currents carefully. "I think it is a floater, the one that passed us."

"Coming back?" I shrank against the cliff side.

"No, it isn't moving at all."

I relaxed a little. "Perhaps locked into a floater dock?"

"Perhaps. Yes, I think so."

"Then we must be near the Vortex Chamber." She sensed my growing excitement.

"Are you going to take the floater?" (This promised some interesting throat-cutting; she was ready.)

"I don't know yet. First, I would like to explore the minds here to see if they know where Beatra is. Second, I am very curious about this so-called Vortex."

"I think you are forgetting why we are here. Kill the guards. Get the floater, rescue your lady friend, and then let's get the Hades out of here."

It was hardly the time or place to argue that the Vortex of Dis might prove central to our entire rescue operation. For the moment, though, it was no more than a vague intuition on my part. So I simply replied, "Let's move on."

Very slowly and cautiously we rounded a bend in the cliff side.

Virgil stopped. "There it is."

I took her eyes. There it was, indeed. The floater was tied up to a little landing dock, carved out of the cliff side. There seemed to be a door opening on the dock, with a couple of windows in the cliff face. *On the opposite side of the chasm.*

We were on the wrong shore.

Virgil shrank back. My stomach at first sagged, then tightened. I could not see the river, but I could hear it, crashing and racing in the canyon below. So could Virgil. The war-spirit drained from her heart. She said bleakly, "You might as well kill me right now. I am not going into the water again."

"Oh, be quiet. Let me think." I reached out across the chasm, searching for the minds of these people. There were six, presently all grouped together. Two—the colonel and his aide—I recognized right away as having been in the searchfloater as it passed us at the falls. The other four men seemed to be stationed here on a semipermanent basis. The local staff consisted of a corporal (in charge), a radio man, a technician-maintenance man, and a weapons expert. A floater came in every day or two with food, newspapers, new kine reels, and fresh laundry. The six were presently seated around a table playing cards.

Nobody was thinking about the Vortex Chamber. They gave me no clue as to where it was or what it was. I had to assume it was nearby.

Virgil yawned and sat down. I didn't probe her mind to find out what she was thinking. I knew it would not be complimentary. In her view all this was my fault. And only an utter fool would have selected the wrong shore! But I knew there would be a way, and soon. For time was running out. Just as I was thinking this, a bell rang somewhere, and they all looked up. I got the impression they were looking toward the radio room. I immediately switched to the brain of the radio man. "I will get it," he said. I sensed that he got up, walked a short distance, sat down again, and that he had closed a switch and was leaning forward toward a microphone. "Vortex Chamber," he said.

A response in throaty gutturals formed in the auditory circuits of his cerebral cortex. "Central Intelligence calling Vortex."

"Go ahead, Central."

"Has Ship 218 arrived yet?"

"Yes, sir. It came in half an hour ago."

"Let me talk to Colonel Aksel."

"Yes, sir." And now the radio man called out: "Colonel! C.I. calling you, sir."

There was a mumbled complaint from the direction of the table, and then a new voice on the microphone. "Aksel here."

"Any sign of the stranger?"

"Nothing."

"How are things at the Chamber?"

"Nothing unusual here."

"Thank you, colonel. You might as well bring the ship back."

"Yes." He returned to the table and stood behind his chair. "We have to go back," he announced to the group.

"Just when you are losing," said the radio man.

I sensed that the colonel was taking his jacket from where he had draped it over the back of his chair and was slowly pulling it on.

He must not leave just yet. A plan was forming, but I couldn't sort it all out. I needed a little more time.

"Help me," I signaled quickly to Virgil. "I want you to look for a certain thing. Somewhere, coming out of the side of the building, wherever the radio room is, there ought to be a long metal rod; or perhaps two rods. If there is only one, it will go down the side of the building into the stone work of the dock. That will be the 'ground' for the radio. If there is a second rod, it will be the lead-in for the antenna, and it may reach up to a horizontal wire strung between two poles."

"I see something."

"Wires?"

"A rod. Just one, going into the ground."

"No aerial?"

"I don't see any."

Apparently only the ground waves were effective for radio transmission in these caverns. No matter. The ground wire would suffice. It was located near the side of the quay, and actually ran all the way down the cliff side into the roiling water.

As soon as I located it I formed a rapidly rotating ionized air-cylinder around it, on the cliff side, about six feet down from the cliff edge. Even at this distance, it was surprisingly easy. I was about to try something that I had never done before, and which even the Brothers would probably not consider possible. I was going to induce an electric current into the radio system of this station, and then I was going to modulate the current in a very precise way.

For a moment I became one with the radio system. I was completely and entirely integrated into it.

I was just in time.

Colonel Aksel and his aide were on their way to the entrance port, when I made the radio call bell ring. They stopped. The radio man stepped into the radio alcove and sat down at the microphone. "Vortex Chamber." He moved a switch, and waited. Nothing happened. He moved the switch back. "Vortex Chamber. Come in, please." He moved the switch to receive once more. And waited. "Vortex Chamber. Is anyone calling Vortex? Come in, please." He switched back to receive. And nothing.

He was about to get up, when I made the bell ring once more.

"Vortex. Who is calling us? Come in, please."

No answer.

By now the colonel had entered the alcove. I switched over to read his mind. "Call Central Intelligence," he said. "Ask them what is going on."

That was fine with me.

"Central Intelligence? Vortex Chamber calling. Yes, sir. No, they have not left yet. Colonel Aksel was on his way out when we began to get these strange call-rings. Twice. But when I answered the call, nobody there. Were you trying to call, or is anything coming through your network?"

My unwitting cohort in Central Intelligence came in clearly. "We have nothing here. You seem to have a receiving malfunction, probably due to proximity to the Chamber. Suggest you check your equipment." The voice was clear and distinct, and still had its characteristic guttural overtone. I listened carefully. That voice should be easy to imitate.

The colonel set out once more toward his ship.

I rang the bell again in the radio room.

The colonel hesitated. "Probably another malfunction," he said.

"Sir, you had better wait, just to make sure," said the radio man. He sat down at the bench. "Vortex Chamber. Come in."

"Central Intelligence calling Vortex Chamber." I mimicked that husky voice very well, I thought.

"Come in, Central."

"We have identified your rings."

"Yes?"

"A search party . . . actually a guard and a dog. On the ledge across the river from you. He says he has been trying to raise you for the last half-hour."

"Half an hour? That's odd. We got our first ring less than three minutes ago."

"Well, perhaps a malfunction in his set. Maybe it got wet, or proximity to the Vortex may have caused difficulties. Be that as it may, ask Colonel Aksel to pick them up."

The colonel was standing behind the radio man. "Tell Central I will pick him up. Also tell Central I should have been informed about this foot search in the first place."

After some further acerbic interchange, we both signed off.

A moment later the floater swung away from the platform and moved slowly in our direction. A search beam played briefly on us. Although the beam did not really bother me, I held one arm over my eyes, mainly because I thought it was expected of me, and waved with the other. Virgil lay at my feet, trying to look like a dog.

The craft drew up level with our ledge, rocking a little, then the side door opened. Virgil and I jumped in. Once inside, I borrowed Virgil's eyes and looked around. The colonel had his aide with him. I studied the colonel quickly. Like all the undergrounders I had seen so far, he had big eyes and a dead-white skin. In addition, he had high cheekbones, a resolute mouth, and an erect military bearing. His forehead was set in a half-frown. I read him: here was a man with a very deep and overriding fear and concern. It showed in his mind and in his face. He made great efforts to put it aside, but he was not completely successful. I thought at first that it was simply fear of me and Virgil. In this I soon realized that I had overestimated our impact on him. *We* were not his basic problem. His face was the battleground of a long and bitter self-struggle. But now he had to put all that aside—whatever it was—and deal with me. He and his aide looked us over with interest. I followed the colonel's thought processes carefully. He was much too observant for his own good. Several things about me immediately jarred his sensibilities. He had never before seen a man with such small eyes. For another thing, my uniform was wrong. I wore the gray tunic and trousers of a peripheral guard, whereas I was ostensibly on a mission for Central Intelligence, and should have been wearing a faded blue outfit. Worse, I was wet, bedraggled, and had neither boots nor weapons. The "dog" particularly alarmed him. The guard dogs to which he was accustomed were considerably smaller, and their eyes much larger, and their canine teeth did not protrude outside their jaws. He was an extremely intelligent man, and it took him only seconds to note these things and consider their implications. But he wasn't done. No, not quite.

He took a step backward. And then he said, very carefully and noncommittally. "Greetings." His hand hovered over the open holster of his electrobeam. His companion looked at us wide eyed. He, too, sensed that something was wrong.

I held up my right hand in greeting.

The colonel's hand was now resting on the handle of his pistol. When he spoke, his voice was low, metallic, and filled with menace. "Where," he asked curtly, "is your radio?"

He had picked the one question that could not be answered. If time had permitted, I would have paused to admire his powers of observation.

Virgil signaled to me. "You take the colonel. I will take the other."

I flashed back at her. "Hold on. I don't want them hurt. Not just yet. The colonel is a very unusual fellow. I would like to look into his mind for a little while."

"They are not going to hold still for that."

"Perhaps we can persuade them. Watch it, I'm about to try something."

I had already determined to try a new vortical experiment. If it worked, everything would be fine. If it didn't, things might soon become awkward, for the colonel was in the very act of drawing his pistol.

I willed that a highly ionized ring form about the colonel's neck, and then another around the neck of the aide. Each annulus developed almost instantly, luminous green wheels, spinning and sparkling. The two men did not even have time to be amazed, because the whirling currents set up by the rings threw awry all the neural impulses traveling up and down their spinal columns. They were completely and instantly paralyzed into rigid pillars of flesh, unable even to bat an eyelash. If I kept them this way too long, they would die by suffocation. I stepped over and took their pistols. It was an immense relief to me that I still had my vortectic powers. (Indeed, they seemed stronger than ever.) They would soon come to an end; for so it had been prophesied. But while I had the power I intended to use it to the full.

I recalled fleetingly the calm face of Abbot Arcrite.

Would the ion-rings have surprised him? Somehow, I thought not. This would have been to him a little thing, a bit of predictable adolescent exuberance. This would not have been high on the abbot's ladder of achievements. I knew that he (indeed, all of them) expected a great deal more of me, more even than Beatra's rescue. Something quite incredible, and somehow involving the gods-eye. And therein lay the mystery. For, timewise, I was probably about halfway through my ordeal, and I still had not the faintest idea of what they wanted me to accomplish down here. And I was certain they didn't know, either.

But back to the present.

I dissolved the paralyzing ion-rings. Both men staggered, as though suddenly relieved of a burden, then put their hands to their necks and breathed deeply a couple of times. I waited a moment, then I slipped into the mind of the colonel. "Yes, my friend," I said to him, "I can talk directly to your mind; and yes, I know what you are thinking, though it helps if you actually express your thoughts in words." I watched him with Virgil's eyes as the staggering suspicion hit him.

Ideas and images flashed through his mind. A man falling. The long drop to the river. Crash! A broken back. Monsters fighting, tearing bloody lumps from the broken body. Flesh fragments escaping, vanishing over the falls. But it hadn't happened. Somehow, none of these disasters had happened. This man, this strange man who had just held him powerless, had lived through it all. *"You...!"* he declared. *"You are the fugitive!"*

And I replied orally. "I am the man. Now, please do as I say, or I will kill you both. Do you understand me?"

Between the pain of his aching neck muscles and the concept of mind penetration, the colonel required a moment to concentrate before he replied. "I understand what you are saying, but that's all I understand.

How are you able to do this to us? What manner of man are you? What is this animal?"

"You don't need to know any of that," I said. "You have a pair of handcuffs in your belt. Tell your aide to lie down on his stomach, put his arms behind his back, and then I want you to cuff his hands." I looked at the aide's boots, then at the colonel's. "And pull off his boots."

The colonel gave the necessary instructions, and presently his companion was immobilized, wide-eyed, mute, and soaked with sweat. The colonel eased the man's boots off, and I pulled them on my own feet. They were not a perfect fit, but they were better than nothing.

Next I handcuffed the colonel to his own steering column. He too was perspiring heavily, but was otherwise calm. I looked into his mind. It was about as I suspected. The bodies of the eight guardsmen had been found. The man who had attempted to get on the President's ship was a prime suspect. He was, however, now assumed to be dead. Only the colonel and the aide knew the truth.

While I studied the colonel I considered a curious fact: my powers of vortex formation were stronger in this area than I had ever before experienced. The abbot's map again. I was very close to the strange source of my vortical powers.

I asked the colonel, "What is in your Vortex Chamber?"

There was something almost laughable about the way the curtains began to drop all over the images in his mind. The Chamber must be a very touchy subject!

"You have never been inside the Chamber?" I asked.

"That is correct."

"But you have heard many rumors?"

"The subject is forbidden. I cannot talk about it."

"In a very literal sense, colonel, you are *not* talking about it."

"I am giving you information. And *that* is forbidden."

I smiled. "Colonel, the regulations are hereby suspended. Now, let us return to the inquiry. Your mind reveals rumors of a vortex in the form of a great, spinning sphere. How big is it?"

"I don't know." He probably spoke the truth. But on the other hand he formed a picture in his mind of a great, vaulted room, and in the center was a glowing sphere, perhaps three hundred feet in diameter, hovering a few feet off the floor.

"What is it made of?"

"Great metal disks, all parallel to each other."

"What makes it spin?"

"It sits over a power source buried in the earth itself."

"What kind of power source?"

"I don't know."

"Is there an entrance to the Chamber?"

"There is a door. No one is permitted in or out."

But now the images were fluttering again, a combination of rumors, speculation, and fantasy. The door had opened a few years back. A fellow officer had told it to the colonel. A body had been taken out of the Chamber. A man had walked in. The door had closed again, but while it had been open, the entire interior of the great chamber had been visible; the spinning vortex had been seen, and sitting around it, three or four men. Words formed in the colonel's mind: "Keepers of the Vortex."

It was all hearsay. Nothing direct. But it was fascinating. It was a fair assumption that my telekinetic powers were so strong here because they were generated by the great-grandfather of all vortices, emanating its magic radiation in all directions, and through a mile of rock, even to the surface of the earth, to the minds of the Brothers, who of course had no idea of the nature of the wellspring of their remarkable powers. But enough of that for now.

"Where is Central Intelligence located?" I asked.

Again the flurry of images. But this time the colonel was not speculating. He knew from personal experience. Central Intelligence was two levels above us. It was a collection of prisons, administrative buildings, and police, guard, and investigational offices.

"Why so much repressive activity?" I asked.

"It is the only way to control the revolutionary movement." There was a sardonic, mocking touch to his answer.

"But why would anyone want to revolt?" I asked. "It seems very peaceful here."

"You seem unaware of our basic premise. It is our destiny to leave Dis and resume the government of the United States."

At first, I thought I must have misunderstood certain of the images. "Try that one again."

"Our people will leave Dis. All of us, nearly ten thousand, men, women, and children, will go forth into the land of the sun. And we will resume control of the country."

Well, there it was.

"Have you consulted the existing local surface governments about this?" I asked dryly.

The colonel studied me carefully. I knew he was hiding something. I dipped into his mind, looking for it. But it eluded me. All I could get was something about "Demo revolutionaries," "minority leader," "doomsday capsule." It probably involved a local political plot, and I didn't want to puzzle over it.

He said: "It was all arranged in the beginning. Dis—meaning the District of Columbia—was created long before the Desolation, to house the officials of the federal government and their families, as a place of refuge from nuclear war. The war came, and the Desolation with it. After the radiation waned, we were to emerge once more..."

"...and take over."

"Of course."

"All of that vanished into history, three thousand years ago."

He shrugged. "It has taken that long for the radiation to dissipate thoroughly."

"Meanwhile, things have changed, both above and below ground. Colonel, your people have evolved to meet conditions underground. A few minutes in our sunlight might be very harmful to you. You'd probably have to wear protective clothing or else adjust to a nocturnal life. Furthermore, we sun-devils, as you call us, have our own city governments. We have no need of you. Leave us alone, and we'll leave you alone."

He shook his head, almost regretfully. "No. I'm afraid it's all settled. We're coming out."

My eyes widened in disbelief. These ghostly caverns were peopled by lunatics!

I tried another approach. "Why did the President kidnap the woman?"

"He was leading a survey party. They encountered you and the woman by sheer accident. They intended to kill you, and they thought they had. They captured the woman for two reasons. Firstly, so that she could not report to the surface authorities that they had been there. Secondly, because it has been our practice for several hundred years to abduct selected representatives of the surface culture in order to follow your progress. We bring them here for purposes of interrogation."

"What happens to them after the interrogation?"

"You mean, when we have extracted all pertinent information from them?"

"Yes, what then?"

"We dispose of them."

I dug with savage anguish into his innermost thought recesses. "The woman Beatra... what will happen to her at Central Intelligence?"

I saw the sequence. He did not even have to form the images. She had already been subjected to prolonged routine interrogation in the security rooms of the White House. The second and final phase would now go forward at Central Intelligence: hypnosis, drugs, and torture.

"They nearly always die," said the colonel. He shrugged his shoulders. He knew, and he knew that I knew.

"How long do they last at Central Intelligence?"

"It depends. A strong man might last a week. A woman, two or three days. Some, less."

My first impulse was to force him to pilot us immediately to that horrid place.

But I no longer had the advantage of surprise. Even though they thought I was dead, the President's person had been threatened, and the patrols on the streets and in the guardposts were probably doubled and quadrupled. And worst of all, the entire complex that constituted Central Intelligence was doubtless buzzing with guards like hornets around a broken hive.

They had everything all wrong; yet, for me, it was almost as bad as if they understood the situation fully and exactly.

The colonel sensed my appreciation of my predicament. He directed a thought at me. "Give yourself up. I will recommend leniency."

I smiled at him. "Leniency? For a man eight times a murderer? Not likely, colonel. I am inclined to think that you are an honorable man. But I don't know about your peers. Men charged with the duties of high government office make and break promises as their politics seem to require at the moment. And yet, the concept has possibilities, in several variations. For example, if I gave myself up, knowing they would kill me, could I make it conditional on their first releasing the lady Beatra, alive and well?"

"Who knows? You would have to ask them."

"You don't really think so, do you?"

We had both thought about that possibility. And we had both come to the same conclusion: the simple act of making the proposition would announce my presence here. After that, all exits would be closed to me. They would eventually find me and kill me. *And* Beatra.

I studied my prisoners.

"As a hostage I have no value," said the colonel.

"I know," I said. He and his aide couldn't be exchanged for either Beatra or for me.

He said, "The woman...is she your wife?"

"Yes."

"I am sorry."

"Do you have a wife, colonel?"

"Yes."

He caught the parallel at once. He too was likely to die, and well before I did. It was just plain silly to tell him, "I am sorry."

"Colonel," I said, "to get to Central Intelligence, we could take this ship back up the canyon to the great shaft. Then we could ascend the shaft until we reach the second level. And then we could proceed down the street to Central Intelligence. And there, somewhere, I will find my wife. Is that essentially correct?"

"Except that you would never reach your wife."

"Central is two levels overhead?"

"Yes."

"I suggest to you, colonel, that there is a more direct route. I suggest that there is a stairwell connecting the inner sanctum of Central with the Vortex Chamber."

"I never heard of it. No, I don't think so."

"Think, colonel."

In my own mind, logic required it. I persisted. "Think back. What are your traditions? Wasn't the Chamber built before Central Intelligence was organized?"

"Yes," he said, "I believe the Chamber was built first."

"And Central Intelligence was later?"

"Very likely." He was curious now himself. "What are you driving at?"

I hurried on. "The first building built at Central Intelligence. Think hard. I suggest that it was not a prison. I suggest that it was simply a guardhouse."

"A guardhouse? To guard what?"

I did not tell him. Perhaps I had told him too much already. I gave the answer to myself. To guard the shaft that went down to the Vortex Chamber. There had to be a shaft, and a big one, because freight-carrying floaters had to have ready access to the Chamber. This was the only way to get the great metal plate sections into it. After the Vortex was completed, the shaft was probably closed to traffic, and then over the years, the original function of the guardhouse was forgotten. It became just another building in the spreading cluster of buildings that became Central Intelligence.

It was just as well the colonel did not fully realize what I was going to propose.

I took from the colonel's brain the directions for finding the door to the Vortex Chamber. It was quite simple. Proceed to the end of the main corridor here in the guardhouse, and there it would be.

It was time to get moving. The radio would have to be knocked out. I formed a heat-ball and struck the ground wire, which promptly melted with a green flash. Then I set the floater in motion, and we slowly recrossed the canyon to the guardhouse dock. I touched the minds inside, one after another. They were all still playing cards in the game room. They did not know we had returned.

The thought formed in the colonel's mind, "What are you going to do?"

"With you, you mean? I have not yet decided. First, I'd like a few more facts about the river. How far downstream does it go?"

"A couple of miles. Then the canyon pinches off, and the river drops out of sight."

"Where does it go when it drops out of sight?"

He shrugged his shoulders. "Who knows? Perhaps into the bowels of the earth."

"If it did that, it would flow on to molten rock, far, far below."

"I do not know about these things."

"Have you ever heard of the Spume?"

"The . . . *what?*"

"The Spume. A vast column of steam blasting from a hole in the earth. It would be perhaps ten or fifteen miles from here."

"No. I have never heard of the Spume."

It all fitted together. In ancient times the Tomack River flowed a long way to reach a great city, some say Washton, and then it flowed on past this city, and emptied into a great bay. The Desolation changed all this. The great city disappeared. A lake stands there now. The sea arm of the great bay vanished. And the Tomack went underground and disappeared. I was the only one in the world who knew its final fate. "Our Tomack River," I said, "goes underground and becomes your Lethe. And when your Lethe has its fatal meeting with molten rock, far below, it all changes to steam and comes to the surface again."

"As your Spume."

"Exactly." I thought of the Returner. He had ridden down this Lethal water, had been hurled down, down, down, in that crazed drop. And then the explosion of cold torrent on molten mother rock, and then the devastating journey upward again, tossed like a pebble in the superheated steam column. How had he survived, even long enough to tell his tale to the monks? He was fantastic. I wished that I had been able to know him.

The colonel had turned pale. He had caught some of the images: a floater in the river, then down the great crevasse toward the earth's center, then in the Spume column. "Is *that* the way you are going to kill us?" he whispered.

I smiled. "Colonel, you are a strong man, and a brave and resourceful one. You might even survive such a trip. But no." Here, I went mental again. "No man who harbors such treacherous thoughts concerning his own government can be completely my enemy." I thought very briefly about enlisting his aid in my search for Beatra, but I decided against it. The risks were too great. In this particular matter he might choose his government over me. Yet, the thought kept coming back to me, a persistent, throbbing warning: don't kill him. So, rightly or wrongly, I made the choice. These two would live.

18. THE VORTEX CHAMBER

WE RETURNED AND entered the post. No alarm rang. Nothing happened. I was already in the main corridor, and with Virgil's eyes I could see the door at the end. The gateway to Beatra.

The game room was midway down the hallway, and I could see that the door was partly open. I considered our chances of sneaking past the game room and reaching the Vortex Chamber portal unnoticed. It was certainly worth a try. We moved silently up the hall. I kept a mental net thrown over the minds of the players, alert for any sign that any of them was watching the door.

We had just tiptoed past when the man on the far side of the table looked up. He was not really looking at the door, and I thought for a moment that the tiny flash of movement would not really register on his conscious mind. A foot past the doorway, we waited, while I focussed back on him.

The thought formed in his brain: "Did I see something?" He stood up from the table and pushed his chair back. And now the others were looking at him inquiringly. He pulled the pistol from his holster and started toward the door. "I think I saw something," he said, "in the hall."

One of the group laughed. "Translation: you are winning and want to quit the game."

Now he was walking toward the door.

I signaled to Virgil. "Close your eyes." I did likewise, and then in swift sequence I threw my arm over my eyes, formed a very large and very bright light-ball, kicked the game-room door fully open, and moved the light-ball into the room.

Immediately afterward, the guard's pistol dropped to the floor, and there were howls of anguish as the men attempted to cover their faces. Virgil and I left them groping for the doorway and calling out to one another, and we proceeded to the end of the corridor.

Here I noted quickly that there was no handle on the door. Just as the colonel had said, it could be opened only from the inside. This was both good and bad. It was good, in that it could probably be opened by the simple turn of a knob or handle on the inside door panel. It was bad in that I would have to take time to locate the mechanism. Obviously, it should be at a conventional height, and at the side of the door. And obviously, the mechanism had either a bar handle or a conventional turning knob. However, I wondered if I had the skill to form and maneuver an air vortex on the other side of a heavy metal door, completely out of sight.

I would soon know.

I gathered all the force of will at my command and brought an air sphere into existence on the other side of the door. I held the palm of my hand against the door, and pressed my ear against it, just above my hand. I made the air-ball bounce a couple of times against the door on the other side, just to make sure it was there. Next, I moved it to where I thought the doorknob

should be, if there were one there at all. Again, I felt
that the air-ball had encountered something. A knob? I
would soon know. I tried to center the whirling sphere
around the knob. And then I tightened the grip of the
ball about the knob, and let it turn. There was a
gratifying *click* in the latch mechanism. I put my
shoulder to the big bronze slab and pushed. It moved
slowly, silently, inward.

We were just in time. A guard, less injured or more
dedicated than the rest, was groping his way down the
corridor toward us. He could not see us, but his pistol
was drawn, and he just might try to fire if he heard a
strange sound or touched a strange body.

We stepped inside and closed the door behind us.
The latch caught firmly. And the door jumped slightly
from the guardsman's following shot. It was of no
consequence. For the moment, we seemed to be safe.

We found ourselves on a high circular balcony that
bounded the upper area of an immense spherical room.
A long spiral staircase led down to the chamber below.
There, a great, radiant sphere hummed a few feet above
the floor and cast a soft luminosity throughout the
entire space. It seemed to be motionless, but I knew
that it was in fact spinning, for this had to be the
Vortex.

It spun on an axis slightly tilted, and it occurred to
me that the axis angle was very like that of the earth
with respect to the sun: which is to say, about twenty-
three degrees. I was puzzled for a moment, because the
sound of the great spinning was not louder. And then I
noticed that the entire sphere was encased in an outer
transparent shell, evidently there to permit operation
under a high vacuum so as to minimize air resistance to
the blades. There must have been a hollow tube
running through the shell axis, because a thin, barely
visible beam of red light shone up through the center of
the sphere and struck a strange optical system, whence
it radiated in three directions, each perpendicular to

the other. Each reflected beam was picked up by its own optical receiver in three widely separated areas of the chamber. Of course, I could have had it all backwards. The three beams might not have been reflected. They might have been individually generated, and collected in a collimator after their passage through the axis of the sphere. Either way, it would have to remain a mystery. Despite its many puzzling aspects (what made it spin? what great energy source made it hover six feet above the floor?), I felt a sudden rapport with this great machine. The feeling was the same as when I made a whirling ball of sand, or a globe of light.

As I watched, I noted the figures of two men, seated at control panels near the globe. I surmised at once that there was another man out of sight on the other side, and that they were all spaced equidistant from each other. The Keepers of the Vortex. They all wore dark glasses against the glow of the sphere.

Just then, another man emerged from an alcove under the opposite run of the balcony. He stretched briefly, yawned, rubbed his eyes, put on his dark glasses, then walked over to one of the Keepers. The latter spoke to him in a low voice and pointed to certain dials on the panel. The newcomer pulled a length of paper tape from a drop-pocket in the panel face, and they looked at it together. Finally, the first man yielded his chair to his relief, walked away, and disappeared into an alcove under the balcony.

I understood at once that these men had dedicated their lives to the Vortex. Only death could release them from this room. What great service were they performing for their fellow man that could persuade them to make such a sacrifice?

It was all very mysterious and intriguing. I wanted to probe their minds and find out what the Vortex was all about, but time was running out for Beatra, and I had to press on.

I had noted another door on the opposite side, which might well be the exit we sought. Virgil and I started on around the balcony—and then Virgil whined.

"What is it?" I flashed to her.

"Don't you feel it? The balcony is trembling."

"I don't feel a thing."

"That is because your senses are dull. Look at the Keepers. *They* know it."

And they did indeed seem to think something was going on. The two seated men, including the new one, had risen to their feet and were bending over the control panels. They were watching something intently. The man who had yielded up his seat hurried from his alcove and stood with his companion.

And then I *did* feel something. The balcony vibrated under my feet.

The light shaft of the Vortex sphere flickered, and it seemed to me that the great ball wobbled very slightly on its axis. Instantly, the men at the control panels began to punch buttons and turn knobs, from time to time looking up at their great spinning creature.

It was a temblor, of course. Rather a mild one, but it seemed to have a startling effect on the Vortex and on the men.

I couldn't figure it out. Obviously, the temblors upset the rotation of the Vortex in some way, and the function of the Keepers was to put it back in perfect "spin." But what the Vortex was doing there in the first place, or why it was important to minimize irregularities in its rotation quite escaped me. I had finally encountered the greatest mystery of them all, the point on the abbot's map, the source of our vortectic powers (prophesied soon to cease), and it was more incomprehensible than ever. So be it.

We were probably safe for the moment. Eventually, of course, one of the guardsmen outside would grope his way out on the dock, and there he would find the colonel. And the colonel would come back inside, would not find any trace of man or animal, and would surmise that we had escaped somehow via the Vortex Chamber. And then what would he do? Would he try to get word in to the Keepers? Quite likely. Indeed, that was about all he could do. And then they would tell him they had not seen me, that they had never opened the door, and that would be that. Everyone would be very baffled and upset.

Nevertheless, we couldn't linger. I put my head down, and Virgil and I crept on around the balcony. We had traversed about half the circuit when I noticed that everything had stabilized again below. The red light beams, barely visible, were now as steady as if they had been ruled in red ink on the drafting board. Two of the Keepers were talking casually to each other. Another was walking across the room, toward what, and for what purpose, I could not guess. The fourth was in the act of throwing a piece of paper tape into a waste basket.

At any moment one of them might look up, perhaps to check the three overhead light beams, or to stretch his neck, or for no reason at all. That would offer problems. I knew that these men had to be left here unharmed, so that they could keep the Vortex in good running order, thereby preserving, at least for the time being, my own vortectic powers. Also, I knew (and this, on an instinctive level) that to destroy these men might bring great harm to Beatra. So I could not blind them, even temporarily. Yet they must not be permitted to see me, or know that I had been within the Chamber.

I would have to occupy them once more with their reason for existence—their Vortex. It should not be too difficult. The balcony had not been swept in weeks. I formed a spinning sphere of air along the floor of the balcony corridor, where it picked up a fair amount of fine dust. I sent the globe right into the path of one of the three ceiling light beams. The beam flickered and wavered. And now the Keepers were calling out to one another and rushing to their positions at the console. While they were glued anxiously to their places by this false alarm, Virgil and I crept on around the balcony. At the end of the balcony runway I dissolved the dust-ball.

The balcony exit door opened from the inside. We quickly closed it behind us and found ourselves on some sort of stone landing. Here, the darkness was total, and I used Virgil's eyes. Even her remarkable vision wasn't too good here, because the uniformity of temperature gave little or no sense of objects, perspective, or three-dimensional impressions.

She listened, and sniffed the dank, musty air carefully. "Nobody is anywhere near us," she said. "In fact, I don't think anyone has been in here for a thousand years."

"How much can you see?"

"It looks as though we are near the bottom of a big shaft. We're on a spiral staircase that goes down and up."

I took her eyes and studied the bottom. The lower level of the shaft seemed covered by a haphazard layer of broken stones, rotting timbers, corroded metal rods, and other assorted debris. I looked up, and with her eyes followed the circular path of the staircase, up and up and around and around, until it finally faded into blackness.

"Do you think there might be a guardpost up there somewhere?" I asked her.

"I can't sense anything."

"Let's go on."

And so we proceeded slowly and silently up the winding stairway. From time to time we brushed against clusters of calcite crystals growing out of the walls. There were no echoes. Even the slight sounds of our footsteps were instantly swallowed up in the total gloom. After a time, Virgil signaled. "I can sense that we are coming to the top. Yes, I can see the top of the shaft. It's closed over. There's nobody there."

"Any side corridors where somebody might be waiting for us?"

"I don't see anything."

I made a tiny light-ball overhead and moved it slowly up the central axis of the shaft. The soft light reflected back from the damp, featureless surfaces.

It was exactly as I had surmised from my discussions with the colonel. The undergrounders had dug this great access shaft here many centuries ago, to lower the great sphere plates into the Vortex Chamber. There was no other way to move the heavy equipment into the Chamber. Its duty done, the builders had sealed off the shaft, placed a guardhouse at the upper level, and then their descendants had forgotten that the great hole ever existed. Not that I could finally throw caution to the winds. For the guardhouse had become part of Central Intelligence, and great danger lay at the shaft exit—if in fact there was one. (Exit? There had to be one! For they had Beatra on the other side, and only the gods knew what the undergrounders were doing to her.)

"Come on," I said. I took the remaining steps two at a time, with Virgil not far behind. There was a railed-in landing at the top of the stairway, and inside the landing, flush with the wall, was an exit door with an iron handle. With the light above and behind me, I seized the handle and tested it slowly and with growing strength and pressure. It would not turn in any direction. I brought the light-ball closer and bent over to examine the handle. Of course it would not turn. It had not been used in several centuries. The lock mechanism had had plenty of time to rust and corrode. Lock, latch, and handle were undoubtedly a mass of thoroughly integrated metal oxides.

I stood back. I did not know what to think or do.

Virgil yawned and lay down in glum silence.

I struck the door panel smartly with my open palm. The shaft echoed with a series of hollow slaps that finally faded away.

Virgil looked up.

"The door is some kind of pressed wood-plastic material," I said.

"Will it burn?"

"I don't know."

Could I cut the lock out with a heat-ball as a cutting torch? Technically it ought to work. The question was—what was on the other side? Would guards be waiting for us there?

"Can you hear or sense anything on the other side?" I asked Virgil.

She stood within inches of the door, ears pricked, cocking her head from one side to the other. "I don't think there's anything there."

I formed a heat-ball and began to move it slowly in an arc about the door handle. Clouds of acrid smoke spewed out from the heated area. Virgil sneezed and backed away.

When the arc had been completed, I extinguished the heat-ball and stepped back. I had expected to see an arc cut entirely through the door area around the handle. I saw only a semicircle of carbonaceous crust. The door must be made of some indestructible material! Small wonder it had endured all these centuries!

I restudied the situation.

"It didn't work," said Virgil impatiently.

"No, it didn't work. Perhaps it's just a question of keeping with it. It did seem to char, at least on the surface. There may be a fire retardant in the material. If I had pure oxygen, I'll bet I could make it burn." I didn't have pure oxygen, but perhaps I could find some.

I knew that the Vortex was the source of my

vortectic powers. I also knew that the closer I was to the Vortex, the stronger my powers. Right now, I knew I was very close to the great, spinning orb. I might be able to accomplish something unusual.

Keeping the light-ball above and behind me, I formed a simple vortex of whirling air about two feet in diameter. This I made to spin faster and faster, until I could begin to sense a stratification of the molecules within the sphere. The heavier oxygen molecules were becoming concentrated in the outer shell of the sphere. The lighter nitrogen molecules were collecting in the center. Holding this air centrifuge steady, I formed the heat-ball again and struck it into the door area above the handle. When I judged that it had got the immediate area of the door handle red-hot, I began to move the heat-ball slowly down in an arc as before. This time, however, I followed it with the oxygen ball. And now the results were greatly different. This time there was no smoke. The combustion was absolutely complete. At the end of the arc I collapsed the heat-ball, oxygen-ball, and light-ball. The handle sagged. I touched it . . . it burned my fingers. I placed my tunic on the landing stones, pulled off a boot, and gave the handle a healthy blow with the heel. It tumbled out on my tunic with a muffled clatter.

We both listened, while I pulled boot and tunic on again.

Virgil sniffed. "There is a current of fresh air coming through the hole in the door."

I felt it, too.

I bent down and peeked through the hole. It seemed completely dark on the other side. "Take a look," I said to Virgil.

She jumped up and leaned against the door with her forepaws. "It's a corridor of some sort. Nobody in it."

"Any side alleys?"

"Can't really say. A few yards down there seems to be a door."

"What scents?"

"Traces of people...months old..."

"In the vicinity of this door?"

"No. Nothing this close."

I explored the hallway in search of mental activity. I found no minds at all. It looked as though we could get out without being seen. I put my shoulder to the door and pushed. It did not move. The hinges were locked with rust. I pushed again. I could feel them begin to crack and give way amid screeching and groaning. I stopped for a moment, fearful that the noise would bring soldiers on the run. But nothing happened. There was no sign of life on the other side. I resumed pushing until I had just enough room to squeeze through.

We hurried up the corridor until we came to the side entrance. Here we paused and listened. "Nothing on the other side," said Virgil.

Should we go on, or should we take this side door?

I tested the handle. It was locked, of course. But the knob-latch was simple, and I merely formed an air-ball on the other side, twisted the knob as I had done on entry into the Vortex Chamber, and opened the door.

19. THE BANQUET

THE DOOR OPENED into what seemed to be a storeroom of some sort.

Virgil sniffed. "People have been here recently. Lots of people. And what's more, there's food here. And I'm hungry."

I studied the place with Virgil's eyes. "Seems to be a cupboard of some sort," I agreed. "Bags of flour. Canned goods. Jars. Boxes. And over there is a cold room. The kitchens are probably next door."

Virgil was so interested in the proposition of finally getting a meal that she failed to hear what I heard: the sound of a door opening somewhere. "Down!" I signaled. We ducked behind a stack of wooden crates.

A dim light came on somewhere.

A voice called out. "And don't forget the hank of smoked fish!"

"I got more than I can carry already," complained a youthful voice.

"And hurry up. You'll have to go up to the cabinet room and clear off the dishes and serve dessert and coffee. Take a cart."

"How far along are they?"

"Don't worry about how far along. Just get up there. You know the President can't be kept waiting."

A boy was going to come in here, get a cart, and go to a place called "the cabinet room," and the President would be there. The President. *Him*. Instantly, I knew what to do.

Just overhead I noted a row of big fish steaks hanging from ceiling hooks. Everything I needed was either in front of my face or being brought to me. The fates were being kind indeed. (Or were they just leading me merrily on?) Virgil could not take her eyes off the fish. She drooled and licked her chops, but I refused to accept any messages from her.

That kitchen boy had better be about my size.

He was.

As he came around the crates I struck him with my fist in the base of the skull, and he collapsed. I dropped my guardsman uniform to the floor and stripped the boy's white overalls from his limp body and drew them on. He had a peculiar white hat with drooping earpieces. I pulled it on. It was a poor fit, but it made my face harder to see.

I pulled down one smoked fish for Virgil and another for the cook. "If the boy moves, just growl at him. If the cook comes in, rip his throat out. Stay here until you hear from me."

As she gulped down the fish she managed one sarcastic comment. "And just where would I be going?"

I found a cart on the far side. Fortunately there was enough light without her eyes. I hoped the kitchen area would be similarly lit. If it wasn't, I was in trouble. But I couldn't take a wolf with me to visit the President.

I needed directions on how to reach the dining hall, and I got them easily from the mind of the cook. A service elevator outside the kitchen would lead to a serving room on the floor above. But first I had to get through the kitchen—and past whoever was in it. I pushed the cart through the swinging doors and across the steaming room, toward the elevator. I kept my head down, but I was looking covertly to both sides. The only person I had to pass was the cook. He was turned away from me and was leaning over one of the utensil counters. I tossed the fish onto the counter at his right hand as I passed. He grunted but did not look up. And thereby he saved his life.

And now the odors of cooking and baking brought the sting of saliva to my mouth. The food would probably be much different from what I was accustomed to in the sun world, but after fasting for many hours, I was not inclined to be fussy. I envied Virgil, but I knew that for me food was out of the question for the time being.

As I stood momentarily before the elevator door, looking for the call button, it opened automatically. It was empty, and I pushed the cart inside, turned, and looked for the button panel that ought to be on the inside. I couldn't see anything, and while I was looking, the door began to slide shut.

I watched that rectangle of vague light grow slimmer and slimmer, and I still had not found the button panel. Did these things operate on a different principle from those I had used in New Bollamer? Frantically I scanned each of the four walls—and even the floor and ceiling. But there was nothing. The door was now shut, and I stood there in total darkness, trying to hold down my rising panic. My palms left streaks of sweat as I passed them hurriedly over the eye-level portions of the walls, searching for something—anything—that might control the flight of this dark prison.

It began to move. Was it going up, or down? And where would it stop? I tasted despair. I should have gotten the whole story from the cook before boarding this crazy cage.

As I stood there, helpless—it stopped. Then, slowly,

the door cranked open. Even before the door was fully open I had cast my mental net out ahead of me. I encountered only one mind. The chief bus boy ... actually a middle-aged man. He was waiting impatiently for me outside in the elevator alcove and he was angry.

I was exactly where I should be! The explanation was simple. The elevator ran only between these two floors, and automatically, so there was no need for buttons.

When I came off the elevator the bus boy looked at me in surprise. "What happened to Joyo?" he demanded. And he added mentally, "And what kind of odd-eyed creature are *you*?"

I had already read the concepts as they formed in his mind. He was stupid, but I was afraid to risk replying orally. I held up my hands helplessly.

(Behind me, I took note that the elevator door had closed and that the elevator was on its way back to the floor below. That was reassuring. It would make it easy for Virgil to rejoin me when the time came.)

"Can't you talk?" grumbled the chief bus boy. "Oh, never mind. (The kind of help they give me nowadays! Cook and I will have to settle this once and for all.) Just get in there and clear off the table. Do you think you can do that without spilling anything on the guests?"

I held up an index finger as a promise of exemplary performance.

He continued his preparations with what appeared to be some sort of dessert and a couple of carafes full of a brown liquid. "When you finish clearing the table, you can serve cake and coffee. And now I have to get back down to the kitchen."

And so he left. While he had been haranguing me, I had been mind-searching the occupants of the other room.

There were ten or twelve people there, and it was indeed a high-level conference.

They were all dressed very strangely, in clothes like

those on the mannequins in the New Bollamer Pre-Desolation Museum. Which is to say, they wore black trousers, white shirts, black vests, and black jackets. Where the collar fastened in front was a funny little thing that looked like a black butterfly. I understood very quickly that these were ceremonial vestments, worn only for occasions of state, such as this midnight cabinet meeting.

There were odd devices hung on the walls. The one on the wall behind the President was a great golden circular plaque, and on the plaque was a bird of a kind I have never seen. It had a great hawklike bill and its wings were outspread. Clutched in the talons of one foot was some sort of leafy twig, and in the other three jagged things, resembling lightning bolts as drawn by a child. Surrounding the bird was a circle of stars, and on the outside a circle of words, which I had to crane my neck to read: "Seal of the President of the United States." On the opposite wall was a rectangular piece of cloth, a pretty thing, with red and white alternating stripes. In one of the upper corners was a crowded collection of five-pointed stars. On a third wall was some sort of map. It showed a generally rectangular-looking area, cut up by dotted lines. I have seen maps before, but this one told me nothing. And finally, on the fourth wall were two big scrolls, side by side. One said, "In God We Trust." (Which, of course, was reasonable, and hardly admits of argument or disagreement.) The other was illegible, or perhaps in some strange language. It said, "E pluribus unum." Now what could that mean? It was all very strange.

There was a lively discussion going on. I caught several words and concepts repeated over and over again. "Doomsday capsule." The colonel's mind had held the same concept, and here it was again. "Emigration." That must mean the great exodus to the surface that the colonel had mentioned. "Quake." That was a new one. Some things I thought I understood.

Some, I knew I didn't. And although I hadn't yet picked up a thorough background of the discussion, I had confirmed one very important fact: my mortal enemy, the President, was here, and he was having a cabinet meeting.

Very respectfully I walked over to his side and took his dinner plate, his salad dish, his bread dish, and all of his silverware except his cake fork and his coffee spoon, while I studied him and probed his mind.

I judged him to be in his late thirties. He had blond, well-trimmed hair. The flesh of his cheeks looked soft and pale. He laid his fork on his plate with long, elegant fingers and leaned forward confidently in his high-backed chair in a position of great poise and personal presence.

"Let me sum up the White House position," he said.

I couldn't make out all the words, but I followed the concepts easily. I put his dishes on the cart and moved to the man next to him.

"We must leave our home here," continued the President. "The temblors are increasing in magnitude and frequency. The Keepers tell me the Vortex has very nearly reached its limit. For nearly three thousand years it has been faithfully absorbing the energy of the temblors and reradiating it harmlessly through the ceiling rocks. We owe our lives to the Vortex. But it has now reached the limits of its capacity."

Now it all began to hang together: the fish tank in the first guardroom that I had encountered. And the mobile hanging in the guardroom. They were crude but effective means for detecting earth tremors. These people lived in hourly dread of movements of the surrounding strata.

He continued. "We have four hundred floaters, loaded, waiting to go up through the grotto route. They line the streets and corridors there. Our storage warehouses are full and overflowing. We are here now for the purpose of setting the hour of the great emigration."

I thought back to the rows of floaters at the exit of the guardhouse, and the warehouses there, stacked with goods. And now I understood what they meant. They had been put there as part of the logistic preparation for the forthcoming emigration. This had been planned for years. It was sheer coincidence that I had stumbled into it at the very climax. Or was it *all* coincidence? The Brothers had very deliberately put me here. And now I was beginning to understand why.

A man on the other side of the table cleared his throat. He was about to speak. I caught his thoughts. He was the Secretary of War. From the corner of my eye I stole a glance at him. He seemed to be very young for a position of such responsibility. He was barely into his twenties. I looked furtively around the table. The ages were scattered. Some young, some middle aged, some very old. This was not a homogenous group of advisers. What did this youth know about war? What qualified each of them to be here?

And then I remembered. These offices were hereditary. The President was President because his father had been President. And here was the son of the recently deceased Secretary of War. I had a sudden crystalline insight into this so-called government. It was government by an aristocracy whose main purpose was to preserve itself. I could assume that it would tolerate discussion, but not dissent. They differed in age and function. But that was all. All had the same intentness of purpose: a callous willingness to destroy. In this there was nothing to distinguish one man from another. They were faces without faces.

"Mr. President?" said the Secretary of War.

"Mr. Secretary."

"The army would like six weeks' notice. Can the Vortex last that long?"

"I understand that it can, but let's ask the expert."

The President leaned toward the man seated on his right. "Mr. Secretary of the Interior, can you confirm this?"

"We can give you two months with a fair degree of confidence. After that, it becomes very chancy. But why would you need six weeks' notice?"

"It's the doomsday capsule," said the Secretary of War. "The hemolytic material is wind borne. After release into the upper atmosphere, it needs a good two weeks for certain circulation over all the earth, two more to ensure total kill, and another two for the residue to decompose by oxygen, sunlight, and water vapor in the atmosphere. Total, six weeks."

"I don't think we need to kill all life on the surface," observed the Secretary of State. "Just enough to make sure our emergence will be unopposed. We really ought to preserve some sort of labor force up there. My guess is that if we kill half of them, or perhaps even less, we won't have any trouble with the survivors."

The President shrugged. "There is no way to reduce the dosage. If it works at all, everything dies. All over the world."

I had stopped, stunned, and I think my mouth had dropped open. The doomsday capsule ... must be the same as the gods-eye. And it carried a poison capable of killing everything on the surface of the earth. The Brothers were right. This was why they had put me here!

I noted suddenly that the Secretary of War was staring at me thoughtfully. A vague disquiet was forming in his mind. He was thinking, "There is something peculiar about this servant boy. He looks very strange. I have never seen him here before. Should I say anything to the President? But if I did, and my fears turned out to be completely groundless, that would make me look like a fool. Perhaps he looks strange because he is a throwback to our sun-devil ancestors. One still crops up, now and then, after thirty centuries. We put them at menial tasks. That's probably what he is, a throwback."

I closed my mouth and quickly resumed my rounds.

The Secretary of the Treasury spoke up. "I have no confidence in the army's doomsday capsule, anyway. I don't think we should depend on it so totally. How do we know it's going to work at all?"

Across from him, the Director of Science and Technology answered. "We won't know for sure, of course, until we try it. Yet scientifically we can see no possibility for failure."

"But," demurred the Secretary of the Treasury, "the War Department put that rocket into orbit over three thousand years ago. Can the poison still be effective after all that time? Suppose we release the canister from the rocket, and suppose it doesn't work. And suppose we emigrate on schedule. The sun-devils would slaughter us."

"Theoretically, time ought not to affect the poison," replied the Science Director.

"Gentlemen..." The President was speaking.

I was now far enough down the table where I could look back and see the President. He smiled. "Perhaps we can satisfy ourselves on that point, here and now. Our ancestral government made only about one gram of the poison. And nearly all of that one gram is presently in the canister on the orbiting capsule."

"You said, 'nearly all,'" said the Secretary of Commerce. "You mean we still have some left down here?" He sounded nervous, I thought.

"Yes," said the President. "There are exactly three molecules underground. And I have two of them with me tonight." He pulled a tiny vial from his jacket. The light was (for me) poor, and that was all I could make out without stopping to stare—which would have been perilous indeed. I moved my cart along.

The room was instantly silent. I caught waves of fear from several of the banqueters. "Nothing to be concerned about," said the President. He pushed his chair back, got up, and walked over to the side of the room. I noticed there for the first time a small aquarium. "Gentlemen, I think all of us keep pet fishes. As we know, they are sensitive to temblor-foreshocks that otherwise can be sensed only by our most delicate seismographic instruments. Well, here we have a tank with three fishes. Catfish, I believe. They have not been fed today, and they are hungry. There are two gelatin fish-food capsules in this vial. Let's see what will happen." He pulled a pair of pliers from his pocket, grasped the little container gently in the plier jaws, thrust the vial under the water, crushed the glass, and then let pliers, glass, and all fall to the bottom of the tank.

The little fish swam to and fro in a great fright for a few seconds. Then they calmed down, noted the two capsules floating on the surface, and made a run for them. Two of the little creatures got their supper. The third didn't. Immediately the first diner began to struggle and to convulse. It frothed the water with its contortions. Then the second one. In a moment they both turned belly up and floated to the surface. But nothing at all happened to the third. It retreated to a corner of the aquarium and remained there, hungry but alive, flat on the bottom of the sand layer, its tiny antennae quivering delicately over its head.

"That may give you a rough idea," said the President. "One molecule per capsule. And as you saw, one molecule was quite sufficient. It enters the bloodstream by being absorbed through the stomach. It immediately begins to catalyze the destruction of hemoglobin. The resulting fragments of the blood cells then traitorously work on the decomposition of their neighboring sister cells. The effect builds up, and it is all over in seconds. The blood can no longer carry oxygen, and the creature simply suffocates."

"I thought you said something about three

molecules," said the Vice President. "Apparently one fish escaped."

"Yes," said the President, "one fish escaped. But only temporarily, I think." He smiled. It was a cruel smile. I knew what he was thinking, and exactly how he wanted to use the third molecule, which apparently he kept in a vial in his safe. He was saving it for a member of this very cabinet, absent tonight, a traitorous revolutionary, a man he identified in his own mind as the Minority Leader, presently on military duty.

Of course! The colonel!

The revolutionaries were against activating the circling capsule. Colonel Aksel was their leader, and I gathered that very recently he had been unmasked by Central Intelligence.

I felt weak. He was the only possible ally I had in this dim place, and I had handcuffed him to the steering wheel of his floater. Well, it was unfortunate, but regrets were futile. I returned to the problem at hand.

"How many molecules are in the doomsday capsule?" demanded the Secretary of the Interior.

"About ten to the twentieth power," said the Chief of Chemical Warfare. "Enough to wipe out the entire population of land-running chordata in the upper world, one hundred times over."

"Land creatures only?" said the Secretary of Commerce. "How about the fish? We've just seen it kill two fish...?"

The Secretary of War smiled. "It hydrolyzes—decomposes—almost instantly in water. It was protected from hydrolysis by a gelatin capsule in the President's demonstration. The fish got it before the water did."

"But how about the water in the fish's blood? Wouldn't that decompose the molecule?" asked the Secretary of Commerce.

"The salinity of the blood strongly inhibits hydrolysis," said the Chief of Chemical Warfare.

"Won't there be a lot left over when we get up there?" said the Vice President. "In the air and on the soil?"

"No," said the Secretary of War. "The material will have a surface life of only six weeks. Fortunately, the last traces will be decomposed by sunlight, oxygen, and atmospheric water vapor within that time. There is nothing to fear."

"What's to keep this deadly stuff from filtering down into our own air system during those six weeks?" someone demanded.

"We have already closed off all of our air contacts. We anticipate no exposure here by air intake."

"But how do we live when we reach the surface?" continued the Attorney General plaintively. "Our food can't last forever."

"By the time we leave here," said the Secretary of Agriculture, "the effect of the poison will be completely dissipated on the surface. It will be perfectly safe to plant crops on the surface."

Every one of them was indeed afraid and concerned—but only for their own skins. It meant nothing to them that they were going to murder every human being aboveground; indeed, every warm-blooded creature that moved on the face of the earth.

"We cannot stay," said the President flatly. "The Vortex was built centuries ago to drain off earthquake energies from our lower strata. It sits now at the apex of a slowly folding anticline. The rate of folding is now becoming so great that it is rapidly reaching the limits of the Vortex to reradiate the vast amounts of temblor energy. When it reaches its limit, the strains in the anticline will give us a quake of Richter eight or nine. Even a small quake would suffice to drop Dis into the river." He looked bleakly about the group. "Further delay is unacceptable. The capsule will be activated tonight."

For the last ten minutes I had been falling into one

shock after another. (Small wonder I had not spilled hot coffee on some august head!) The so-called United States of America was going to emigrate to the surface within a few weeks. So I should immediately rescue Beatra and get us both topside, and warn my fellow surface citizens. Except that that would be all wrong. Because the poison in the gods-eye—or doomsday capsule—would be unleashed in a matter of hours, and everyone up there would die, including Beatra and me, if we were successful in escaping.

By now I had cleared the table, and I was beginning to distribute the desserts—which seemed to be some sort of frozen cakes. While all this was going on, I had been probing these minds for additional information.

From the mind of the President I had learned Beatra's whereabouts. She was, in fact, under interrogation in a high-security cell block not far away on this same level. I thought I knew how to get there. But I didn't want to leave just now because I was discovering things that affected the historical future of life both above and below ground. It would be pointless to rescue Beatra and return with her to a dead world.

So Phaedrus' prophecy was finally clear. One civilization would live, and another would die. Dis would live, and everything above would die. And that wasn't all. Possibly I would bring Beatra out. But safely? I would bring her out to die before another cockcrow. As would I. And every other living creature.

The alternate would be to take her to a hiding place somewhere here underground, until it was safe to go to the dead upper world. Even if this were possible, it was a thought too traitorous to contemplate. If our world was destroyed, we would die with it.

But we weren't dead yet. I had searched the mind of the Chief of Chemical Warfare, and I had learned the location of the control room for the doomsday capsule. It, too, was here in the Central Intelligence cluster.

I poured a last round of coffee, and then brought liqueurs and cigars. (How was it possible to grow tobacco underground!)

And now I was finished here. To stay longer would invite suspicion. And so I would leave.

I paused to think a moment. The streets and corridors, especially those leading to the grotto, were swarming with guards. I not only had to destroy the doomsday capsule control room and rescue Beatra—I also had to get out with her, and safely.

To top it all, my vortectic powers were due to fade away within a few hours. I had no clock, and there was no way to keep track of the time, but I knew I would have to hurry.

It was time to act.

The President was just lighting his cigar, when several things happened. I moved behind him and formed a big light-ball over the table. He threw his hands over his face—as did they all—stumbled to his feet, and pulled a pistol from inside his tunic. I put my arm around his throat and stuck my own pistol into his spine. "Drop it," I whispered. The accent might have seemed strange to him, but he got the message explicitly.

He dropped it, gurgling.

I pulled him through the blinded, groping men to the elevator alcove.

20. THE CONTROL ROOM

I CONTACTED VIRGIL. "It's time to join me again."

"I'm still hungry."

"Forget it. Come through the kitchen. Right outside the kitchen you'll find an elevator. That's a smallish metal room that will take you straight here. You get on, the door closes, the elevator comes up one level, stops, the door opens, and I'll be here waiting for you. Come on! Hurry! I don't know how long I can keep the people here under control."

"I think there are some people in the kitchen."

"Smile sweetly at them."

"Here I come."

In a moment I heard the clanking of cables in the elevator shaft. Next, the door opened, and Virgil came bounding out, tail wagging. "Who's *he?*" she demanded.

"This is the President of the United States. Treat him with respect, because he is going to help us get into the Control Room, and then find Beatra, and then he's going to help us get out of here."

I had taken my arm from his throat, and was pushing him along the corridor.

He rubbed his adam's apple with one hand and his eyes with the other. He was still blinded. "Who are you?" he demanded hoarsely. "How did you make that light-thing? What do you want?"

"I am called Wolfhead."

"What?"

"I am he who seeks the kidnaped sun-devil woman."

He was silent a moment. "Ah yes. So you are the one. You were on the tongue-board of my floater. We thought you died in the river. Are you her husband?"

"Yes."

"So you are not one of the Brothers, and yet you have these strange powers. We thought only your monks were able to utilize the Vortex radiation for telekinetic displays, and even then only after long training. Most interesting. I can see that we will be forced to bargain with you. You have come for your wife? Well, you can have her. You are both free to go."

I was silent. He expected, of course, that I would be happy to leave with Beatra, and that I did not know we would both soon thereafter die by the doomsday capsule. How to accept his offer of Beatra and destroy the capsule simultaneously? There had to be a way. We continued to walk down the corridor. It was dark, and I used Virgil's eyes.

"Several people approaching up ahead," she warned. "I smell metal. Guns, perhaps."

"How many?"

"Four."

"That's fine. We can use them." I dipped into the mind of the President. "One of your patrols is coming. Do exactly as I say or I will splatter your spine forty feet up the hallway."

"Of course."

"It is simple. Just tell the corporal you want the patrol to accompany us to the doomsday control room."

He hesitated.

"Your choice, Mr. President." I jabbed the pistol muzzle hard into his back. He jerked with pain.

"All right." His voice shook.

The patrol came into clear view. The corporal saw us approaching. He barked an order. The four of them quickly unslung their rifles and the corporal called out again, this time to us: "Halt!"

"Corporal!" cried the President. "Put your weapons away, and approach."

"Mr. President! Sir! I did not recognize—"

"No matter, corporal. I want you to accompany us for a short distance."

"Of course, sir!" He looked at me, then at Virgil. I stood slightly behind the leader of this godforsaken land, and my weapon was still pressed into his back. I searched the mind of the corporal in an effort to determine whether he understood I held a gun. He did not. He was too full of surprise and wonder at his leader's bizarre entourage: kitchen boy and the biggest, fiercest-looking dog he had ever seen in his life. The three guards of his little patrol were likewise more astonished than suspicious.

I followed the mental map in the President's mind, and within five minutes we turned a corner in the corridor and approached a *cul-de-sac* guarded by still another patrol. Their leader watched warily as we approached. I gave the President his instructions, and he passed the word to our corporal. "Go on ahead, corporal, and tell them we are coming."

"Yes, sir." He took off, double time, up the corridor. In a moment he trotted back. "I told them who you are, sir."

"Thank you, corporal."

The standing patrol let us through.

We stood before the door.

And now I had several problems. It was no longer possible to keep the guards in front of us. They were now on either side, and they could see that I had a pistol stuck in the back of their President. The corporal of the standing guard was the first to notice.

Oh, I read him clearly! His first reaction was total astonishment; his second was to jump on me and take the pistol away by brute force. And then, a fraction of a second later, he realized that I would have time to kill the President.

"Tell him," I instructed my hostage, "that he and his men must drop their weapons. If they make any sudden movements, you will be the first to die."

"Yes," said the President huskily. "Drop your weapons," he told the corporal. "I have been taken prisoner. I order you not to attack this man."

I commended him. "Well done." And that led me to my next problem: how to open the door.

I knew, by searching the President's mind, that only two people in this entire underground city had access to the control room: the President and the Secretary of War. Except it wasn't quite that simple. There was a slot in the center of the door, designed to accept a small metal plate, coated on one side with magnetic iron oxides in a specific pattern. The other side of the card was highly polished and was designed to receive a fresh thumb imprint. And the President had left his identoplate locked in his desk in the Oval Office, back at the White House.

He smiled at me grimly. The thought formed in his mind: "We seem to have reached an impasse."

I did not reply. I was thinking. I could make him call a messenger to open his desk and bring the plate. On the other hand the Secretary of War was undoubtedly closer; but did he carry *his* plate on his person? Probably not. Perhaps I should make the President send all these soldiers to the White House for the presidential plate. Good way to get rid of the soldiers. Only temporarily, of course, for a whole battalion would soon return. Any way I did it, in ten minutes the whole city would know I was *here*, at the jugular vein of their emigration plan, with an electro at the spine of their beloved President. He would therefore have to come along with Beatra and me—else our lives wouldn't be worth a clipped florin.

He continued. "I suggest we leave this place immediately and proceed to the interrogation rooms. There you can take your wife, and you will be given safe conduct to the surface."

... where we would continue to enjoy life for not more than a couple of days, I thought.

"There is a phone on the wall," I told him. "Call the interrogation officer. Tell him to stop the interrogation and to give her whatever medical treatment is necessary."

The corporal and the President had a brief exchange, then the President picked up the handset and entered into a short dialog with persons unseen. I followed the President's part of the conversation and was satisfied that his instructions would be followed. "Get a report on her condition," I said.

He shrugged his shoulders. "You understand, the interrogation was pretty well along."

My voice was ice-cold. "You mean they have already begun the torture?"

"I don't know." He was sweating heavily. I read his mind. He really didn't know. But he suspected...

I began to sweat with him. "Get a report."

There was another short conversation. He looked up at me. I could see the fright in his eyes. "There is some residual pain, but she will be sedated, and the long-term prognosis is good." His mind was blurred by fear. I couldn't read him clearly. But he believed she was still alive. (Or was that merely what *I* believed? Well, then, that's what I believed. For now. It had to be good enough. I could still get her out of here and get her to the monks. They could bring her back to health.)

"You had better hope she is alive and in good condition, Mr. President." I turned back to the door.

It was at that instant of turning that my gun hand was struck. I tried to react. I tried to pull the trigger on the pistol that would kill the President, and I think it actually may have moved a little. But the paralysis spread immediately from my hand into my arm and then over my entire body. Even as I stood there, feeling like a frozen idiot, I realized what had happened. This was the most heavily guarded door in all Dis. It was even more taboo than the entrance to the Vortex Chamber. It would of course have overhead, TV-guided guns. Guards in another room had been watching us through closed-circuit TV all along, and they had fired as soon as they thought they could get a clear shot at me without endangering the President. Virgil went down in a sprawling heap almost at the same instant. From the way she dropped, I assumed she was dead.

I was in the very act of trying to form a light-ball, something that would at least blind the spectators, visible and invisible, when the second beam hit me. I think it was meant to kill me, and the only reason it did not was because at that instant both the floor and ceiling shook from a mild temblor, throwing me off balance and disrupting the sighting mechanism of the ceiling pistol. The second shot simply seared my leg. But it was enough to make me lose consciousness. As I fell, I thought, well, this is the end. I had done my best, and I had come very close, but I had failed, and now they would get on with killing Beatra. And me. And the world above.

21. The Poison Canister

I AWOKE GROANING, in total darkness. It took me a long time to reorient my thoughts. I lay on my back on something pliant. A mattress laid out on the floor, perhaps. Not important. I tried moving my arms. They were free. And so were my legs. "Virgil?" I whispered mentally. No reply. They had probably killed her.

And why hadn't they killed me?

I heard low voices.

I reached out in mental alarm and touched minds. One was saying: "I think he is awake." Another: "We must tell him immediately that he is among friends."

The third said, "Stranger, do you remember me? Do you need more light?"

I recognized the mind. It was the colonel! I had locked him to the steering wheel of his floater. Evidently he had got loose. Anyway, here he was. I was glad. "A little more light would help," I said. "Do you have a light source here, or should I make a light-ball?"

Someone spoke up hastily. "We can provide the light. We have heard that your light-balls can be quite devastating."

The ceiling took on a dim radiance, and I was able to see my surroundings. The colonel stood at the side of my pallet, hands on hips, studying me gravely.

I got a good look at him, probably for the first time. In the beginning, when I was killing underground guards with a right good will, they had all looked nearly alike to me, with their strange white faces and their great owl-eyes. But differences were beginning to emerge, and the colonel was a case in point. His face showed character. There were lines on his brow and at the corners of his eyes, and his jaw had a firm set. Some people, including perhaps even myself, would instinctively trust him. And yet I could see that certain others, such as high government officials, might react in opposite fashion.

I shot a question at him. "My wife?"

"There has been no change since the President reported her situation to you. At that time, he ordered treatment for her recovery. So far, he has not countermanded the order. We believe he simply forgot her. Nevertheless, we consider that she is still in great danger. But we think you would both be in even greater danger if you were both able to return to the surface right away."

"Because of the doomsday capsule?"

"Precisely."

"How about the wolf?"

"As in your case, the temblor saved her from a direct hit. For a time she was in deep rigidity, which is to say, her heart was in spasm and her lungs paralyzed, but we connected her to an exterior oxygenated blood pump, and now she's recovering nicely in a nearby room. She is a very strong animal, and we think she'll be on her feet in half an hour."

"How did you get us here?"

"The disposal squad that picked up your two bodies was led by one of my men."

"Well, then, *why...*?"

The colonel's brow wrinkled. "Why did I save your life? That's easy. We're basically on the same side. A pity we didn't have more dialog before you fastened me to the steering column of my floater. Like you, I am now under a death warrant. I think we should work together."

"How?" I said cautiously. "I thought you were all for the great emigration."

"True. We have to leave here, and soon. The thing I'm against is the use of the doomsday capsule. It's barbarous even to think about it."

"Ah, I think I begin to see. That's why the President calls you a traitor."

"Yes. I am the Minority Leader of the Democrats— the Demos. We are indeed traitors to the President and to the Administration. But to our country? Never!"

The colonel was an idealist. I was not so sure that the people of Dis would be welcomed with open arms on the surface. Our East Coast was already becoming crowded, with nearly a million people squeezed between sea and mountains. But on the other hand, I knew we wouldn't try to kill them *en masse*, either.

"Very well, then," I said. "At least you're against the capsule, and certainly so am I. But I also want to get out of here with my wife. How can we work together? Can you get to the doomsday control room?"

"Perhaps we don't have to."

"Then what do you have in mind?"

"Consider the mechanism on the capsule. Three operations are necessary. First, the computer in the control room has to give instructions to the capsule to tumble one hundred eighty degrees so that the retro-rockets will face forward. Next, the retros are given the order to fire. This causes the capsule to descend to the correct height. Finally, the capsule opens, and the cargo drops into the upper-air currents."

I followed these very graphic mental pictures in his mind. "Yes?"

"That is the normal sequence. But there's a way to stop it before it begins."

"How?"

"In case the capsule machinery malfunctions before the sequence starts, the rockets will simply fire in their present rearward position and the capsule will immediately enter an escape spiral that will send it into the sun."

"And I suppose you know how to make it malfunction?"

"We think *you* can do it."

But for the pain in my cheek muscles I would have laughed. "Colonel, I can do little magic tricks within a few dozen yards, but that thing is two hundred miles up!"

"Four hundred fifteen at apogee, two hundred thirty at perigee," he said. "Nevertheless, if you could get inside it, mentally, I mean, you might be able to close a relay, short a fuse, cause a major oxygen/hydrogen leak, any one of a number of things."

I shook my head regretfully. "Gentlemen, I am afraid my powers are subject to the inverse square law of radiation. At that distance I couldn't harm a fly."

The colonel persisted. "Within the hour, we expect a transit directly overhead. This means you will have the great strength of the Vortex at your command for several seconds."

Is it possible? I thought about it. "I would need to have the Vortex directly under me," I said.

"We can arrange it."

"You might have to forego quake protection for that several seconds."

"We think a few seconds will not matter."

"This Vortex," I asked. "Just what is it, exactly?"

"It is quite a story," said the colonel.

"I'd like to hear it." This was my great opportunity to unmask this greatest of mysteries.

"Very well then. Let me start with a simple geologic fact.

"Earthquakes are caused by movements of the great continental plates, and occur almost exclusively at the leading edge of the moving plate. For the continent of North America, the leading edge is twenty-five hundred miles away, to the west, and there they do have great quakes, caused by the collision of the great western plate with the Pacific plate. But there is nothing like that here on the East Coast. The eastern, trailing edge of the continental plate is receding from the Atlantic plate, not colliding with it. In the decades before the Desolation, when our ancestors were preparing Dis, they foresaw no danger from earthquakes.

"But then the Desolation came. The great bombs left vast, empty craters where cities used to be. The physiography of the eastern seaboard was changed. Hills, valleys, lakes, and bays were created where none had existed before. The earth's crust was unbalanced. To equalize and relieve the strains in its new surface profile, the crust began to settle and shift. And then we discovered that Dis had been built over an anticline, a rock fold that had been formed and stabilized back in the Miocene, twenty-five million years ago. And that it was now becoming unstabilized. We couldn't leave. We couldn't return to the surface. The radiation was still lethal, and would remain deadly for another twenty-seven hundred years. We couldn't dig away from the area of the anticline: it dominated the entire seaboard. We were becoming reconciled to doom when one of our greatest scientists proposed the answer: seize the nettle, grasp the thorn. In a word, scrape off the overburden from the anticline at its highest and weakest point, and build there the great Vortex, tuned to be suspended and rotated by the energy poured into it by temblors and latent quakes. The Vortex drains away energy from the anticline as fast as it is generated. Hence no quake-forming forces are allowed to accumulate within the anticline. The Vortex transforms this energy into new wavelengths of electromagnetic radiation. Like cosmic rays and neutron rays, this radiation passes through miles of rock. It meets all our heat requirements, and it renders our very walls luminescent. It is indeed our source of all energy. I understand that certain human mutants, sun-side, called the Brothers, are able to utilize this energy in strange ways. It is curious, I might add, that no one within Dis has similar talents. We think this is because we were never exposed to the overland radiation necessary to develop the mutation.

"But now our great Vortex is approaching overload, and we must leave here or die."

"Can't you build another Vortex?" I asked.

"The question was debated many years ago. They decided to emigrate instead. And now it is too late to do otherwise."

We were silent a long time. The colonel had indeed explained a great deal—everything except why my vortectic powers were due to cease within hours. I was about to ask him about this, when he said: "Speaking for the Demos, I have a favor to ask."

"Say on, Colonel."

"If we are successful in aborting the poison canister, you and your people will owe me some slight return."

"We will indeed."

"Then, tell your people that we come in peace. Tell them that we offer them no threat, but quite the contrary, we can offer to them all the technology of the ancients. Things they have not been able to rediscover, we learned in our infancy, and we are ready to teach everything. Your people will see us only during your hours of darkness, for we are by the nature of our vision night people. And you need not fear our numbers; we are few, and you are many."

"I think it will be all right, Colonel. Not all of the surface people will welcome all of you, but some of us will welcome some of you, especially those of us who understand that you and the Demos saved our lives."

"Then let us be about our business, for time presses."

"We have no tracking equipment of our own," said the colonel. "However, we have a man on the tracking station at Central Intelligence, and we know that the capsule will be overhead in thirty minutes."

We were climbing a stairway rough-hewn from limestone strata. "We call this the crater," explained the colonel. "Actually, it is two craters, one almost exactly within the other, a strange incident of the Desolation. The bottom crater filled with water, and the water percolated downward, leaching out these caverns and passages. The Demos helped nature, and now we have a passage all the way to the surface."

We were a group of three. The colonel's aide brought up the rear. Virgil bounded on ahead. She could smell wisps of air seeping from the surface, and she was trembling. Beneath our feet less than a thousand yards of rock separated us from the Vortex. Above, darkness lay on the face of the earth, and among the myriad twinkling light points there would soon be one very special one: the capsule.

We paused now before a small trapdoor hinged into the bottom of the tunnel. It was locked with chain and hasp, and the colonel opened it with a key. The little door swung inward. The night air began to flow in. Virgil began to dance.

"Let her go out first," I said.

"Good idea," said the colonel.

And so she went out. I kept in mind-touch with her. She saw nothing, smelled nothing, heard nothing, so we crawled out in single file.

Outside! We were on the surface! I got to my feet, inhaled deeply, and looked around me. The exit was cleverly hidden in a grove of mountain laurels interspersed among scrub pines. Above, in an arc on all sides, swept the rim of the great crater. This was the center of the abbot's map of concentric circles. I knew this place. It was only a few dozen miles southwest of Horseshoe Bay. I had hunted here. And that reminded me. Where was Virgil? I had lost contact. Well, no matter. She was free to go. We had now been underground for nearly twenty-four hours. It seemed like a lifetime, and now we had emerged from a nightmare, even if only momentarily. Virgil had earned her freedom. Her eyes and slashing fangs had served me well, and perhaps I would need her again, but she had opted for release. So be it.

I looked overhead and picked out the circumpolar stars. The Big Dipper. Cassiopeia. The Dragon. And then I found it. The gods-eye... the capsule... dooms-day... Barely visible, best seen by looking a little to one side of it. Like the planets and asteroids, it was not self-luminous, but merely reflected the light of the sun, presently invisible behind the earth.

A point of light, so small, so beautiful—and so deadly.

"Over here," said the colonel quietly. "I have already staked out the exact point where the center line of the Vortex intersects the crater."

We walked across through the brush.

"What will you do?" asked the colonel.

"Just before the capsule draws directly overhead," I said, "I will attempt to form a heat-ball in the control panel." I laughed shortly. "But you understand, I have never before tried to form a heat-ball at such a great distance."

"I know. But you must try. At this very spot in the crater there is theoretically what our technicians call a node—a point of magnified vortical power. There is, in fact, supposed to be a line of nodes extending along the vortical axis, away to infinity."

I said nothing. I simply did not believe any of this. He was sincere in his own beliefs, but he was asking too much from me.

The little point of light suddenly seemed to become brighter.

I dimly noted that the colonel was looking at the space vehicle through a telescope. He stiffened—then he cried out. "Something's happening up there! The rockets! The rockets are firing! We're too late!"

I grabbed the glass from him. It took me a moment to find the thing. And then I caught it. The little ship itself was still just a pinpoint of light. But in front of it there was a vast tongue of flame, and beyond the flame was a growing cone of luminous smoke.

This meant the control room had already commanded the capsule to reverse its position one hundred eighty degrees to bring the rockets forward, and then to fire the retros. The lethal sequence had been started. I could no longer send it into outer space. It would be immune to all interference from here on in, up to and including the moment when it opened its doors to spew out its deadly cargo. There was no way to interfere. Anything I could do now to the control panel was totally irrelevant.

The colonel stood there, motionless, silent. But he did not have to explain what this meant.

And so it had been prophesied. One civilization lives, and one dies.

I began to tremble. Whether from the physico-mental impact of the node, or whether from the realization that earth's history was finally coming to an end, I do not know. The telescope fell from my nerveless hand.

I looked up at the poison-bird. If there were only a way I could get my hands on that death-canister! There had to be some way, there had to be something I could try. I cried out, *"Try!"*

And at that instant I felt a vibrant, tugging power. It swept through my body and my brain in an overwhelming tide. Time seemed to slow. The colonel's face seemed suddenly vacant. He had been saying something, and now his mouth was open, but no words emerged. I looked overhead. The little light was still there, but it had stopped moving.

I *knew*.

I was encountering again the strange phenomenon in which everything around me slowed down, and the universe seemed to be operating in some weird sort of slow motion. I knew from experience that that was not true. The universe was turning away at its regular rate of speed. It was I who had accelerated. My thought processes and muscular movements had been speeded up by exposure to the node, and it had occurred without conscious effort on my part.

As I looked up, I sensed the series of nodes, extending a good three hundred miles and more overhead, straight through the capsule, and beyond. One such node completely enveloped the capsule.

It would not be quite accurate to describe now a *series* of events. The difficulty is that, although it would seem that certain things had to happen before other things could happen, yet the flow of time was so incredibly altered that the next several events did not necessarily occur in logical order.

I was on board the capsule. Perhaps to state it more accurately, some part of me was on board. I remember thinking at the time, this is impossible. This cannot be happening. But now that I am here in the capsule, I will die, because of the cold and the lack of oxygen. I remember looking through the porthole. I could see a patch of stars, and I remember Orion especially. I was looking toward the southern skies. But nothing was moving. Nothing but me. The capsule and the stars were locked in time and space.

I located the handle to the floorboards and lifted them up.

And there it was. A small innocent black box, no bigger than my hand. It was connected to some rather clever machinery. I could see how a clockwork mechanism would automatically open a port in the side of the space vehicle and then the little door on the box would open, and a spring-loaded device would thrust the box contents outside the capsule into space.

So I did a thing, a certain thing, the work of a timeless moment.

Next I had a sensation of falling, bumpity-bump, for mile after mile, as though crashing down an endless ladder and hitting every rung.

And then I was back on the ground, dazed, trembling, nearly frozen, wondering why the colonel was staring at me in horror. No, not at me. At the little black box that I held so casually in my right hand.

"I don't believe it...!" he whispered.

I didn't either. I felt faint, and I knew I was about to collapse.

He reached out and took the poison canister just in time.

22. BEATRA

THE COLONEL HELD the black box with both hands. He looked at me, and I looked at him. He backed off a step. "No," he said.

"I can use it," I said. "Beatra is still a prisoner here. But the entire city is hostage to me if I have the poison. The President will have to let me have her."

"No," he insisted. "You could not exchange the poison for her, for then the President would have the poison, and what he would attempt with it would be quite unpredictable. There is no way that you can make use of it and live. And she would die too. If just a little gets in the air, all here will die. No, we can never use this. It must be destroyed."

I didn't necessarily agree, but I wasn't inclined to take it by force.

The colonel motioned to his aide, who brought him a pail of drinking water. The colonel dropped the canister into the water. It bobbed up and floated inertly. He got a stick from somewhere, pressed the canister down to the bottom of the bucket, then hammered on the stick with his fist. Something gave. This time the box stayed at the bottom of the water. He left the stick in the bucket. "The water will take care of it," he said. "And now we must close up here and see if we can find your wife. What...?"

Startled, we all looked toward the laurel grove.

It was Virgil. "I have come back," she said to me, "because I was seized with premonitions. That piece of your brain within mine speaks of catastrophes soon to occur. I do not know whether I will fare better on the surface, or underground with you. What do you think, Jeremy?"

"I think I need you, Virgil."

"Possibly. But that hardly answers my question."

"I don't know the answer."

"No, you don't know. But a kind of luck pursues you, and the prophecies bespeak your survival. For these reasons it may be better for me to stay with you."

"Then come along, and let's try to be lucky."

The colonel locked up, and we followed him back down the dank, twisted passages toward his floater, parked a couple of blocks down the street.

As we walked along, I put Virgil out in front and took her eyes. We expected no trouble. Nevertheless, I kept throwing my mind-net over everyone who came close to us. I found nothing. A group of workmen returning from a night shift were curious and uneasy about the "dog." An approaching guardsman... wondering what would happen if he did not salute the colonel. But nobody ever found out, because as he drew abreast, he shrugged mentally, and saluted. So did the colonel.

Virgil, the aide, and I got in the floater, and then the colonel got in at the controls and drove us through a back route into the Central Intelligence complex. The route involved only a couple of turns, and I memorized it for possible future use. We parked the ship at the official zone and got out. The aide and I followed the colonel up and down dimly lit halls to the interrogation section.

And now we approached our first checkpoint.

Ever since my "return" from the space capsule I had been aware of a strange phenomenon. My rapport with the Vortex, instead of diminishing after I had left the line of nodes, had increased. I could sense its immense vibrant presence, a thousand feet below.

I tried a bizarre thing. I visualized the great central axis, whirling, whirling. And then I gathered all my willpower, and I "leaned" into the upper part of the thing.

The Vortex shuddered, then broke into a massive, continuing wobble. I could see none of this, yet I knew it was happening. How the Keepers must be scurrying about, checking their dials and gauges, and staring wide eyed at each other!

I pressured the Vortex axis again. This time it leaned farther out. I sensed that the Keepers were now applying all the power in the gyroscopes to force the axis back into a steady vertical spin. I applied still more force. So did they. I wondered who would win an ultimate test of strength. But it was not my present object to find out. I locked in and maintained my present torque against the Vortex axis. I had what I needed.

"Colonel," I said, "I want you and your friends to leave Virgil and me now."

He looked at me blankly. "Why? You are going to need help to find your wife and get her out of here."

"I am grateful for your offer. Especially since it is made at a great personal risk. But for what I have in mind, Virgil and I must go on alone. Your presence would actually increase my danger, and Beatra's."

He shrugged. "As you will. In that case, I will gather my little band of Demos, and I will meet you on the surface."

"Yes. See you topside."

I followed his mind as he walked away with his aide. He kept looking back, fearful for me, puzzled, concerned. Perhaps he was right.

I was now at the checkpoint, and the guard was studying Virgil and me suspiciously.

"Pay attention," I told him. "My name is Jeremy Wolfhead. I am the invader from the surface. I have already killed a number of your people, and I could easily kill you if I wanted to. But I choose not to harm you. Instead, I want you to tell your President that I would like to talk to him."

His cheeks, already ivory, turned an ashen white. Little beads of sweat began to form on his forehead. He leaned forward and spoke with shaking voice into the visibox. "Checkpoint Able. The sun-devil is here with his devil-dog and wants to talk to the President."

I waited quietly while the connections were made. I felt relatively safe. I had already read the guard's mind and I knew there were no overhead electrobeams at this gate. Later on, there would indeed be ways to kill me, but I did not think the President would use these until he satisfied his curiosity as to why I had been fool enough to return.

The next voice on the box was that of the President. It was all done very quickly, and I was both surprised and relieved.

"What do you want?" he said resentfully. Obviously he knew of my rescue by the colonel and the Demos.

"My wife."

There was a brief silence. I had the impression he was whispering with someone. Then he said: "You are very near the interrogation chambers. I would suggest that you proceed to the next checkpoint. You will receive further instructions when you arrive there. This guard will accompany you."

I smiled. He was too far away for me to read his mind, but the guard's mind was wide open. The inner checkpoint was highly guarded. There were overhead rifles and a cluster of police. "Very well, Mr. President," I said. I motioned to the corporal to start out and to walk ahead of me. "You had best leave your pistol here," I told him, "because if you don't, I will kill you."

The thought flickered across his mind that perhaps he could draw his weapon and fire before I could harm him. "No, you can't," I said. "But it might be fun to try, and if you are successful, they might promote you to sergeant."

He unbuckled his holster, laid it on the desk, and we set out.

I explored the minds waiting for us around the bend in the corridor. Six or seven guardsmen. They had already received instructions, and their weapons were out. The rifle butts were pressed against their shoulders and they were taking aim. Not to mention three overhead television electros.

The corporal was becoming more nervous as each step brought us closer to my waiting death. He did not want to get caught in the line of fire.

"Call out to them," I told him. "Tell them I have a very important message for the President."

"Yes, sir!" He put his hands to his mouth and shouted: "Hold your fire! The sun-devil claims he has an important message for the President!"

I sensed a hurried consultation around the corner. After that, the leader, a lieutenant, was apparently on the phone talking to the President. The President ordered them to put their arms down and let me approach the visibox on the guard desk. The lieutenant did not object. Firstly, the orders were straight from the President. Secondly, they both knew that I would still be covered by the overhead rifles. Those rifles were a chance I had to take. I knew the President felt personally safe from me for the moment, and that he was indeed curious as to my message for him.

I approached the box. "I have come to bargain for

my wife and safe passage."

"Bargain?" He laughed. "You are in no position to bargain. I could kill you where you stand."

"You would be running a grave risk, Mr. President. For some moments now I have been synchronized with the Vortex. And for several moments I have been applying a torque to its spin-axis. The Keepers know only that some unaccountable force is being exerted against the Vortex. They have countered my force with an opposite and equal force, applied to the central gyroscope within the Vortex. If I should suddenly release my control, the Vortex would be immediately subject to the gyro counterforce. And that counterforce would overwhelm the Vortex before it could correct itself."

"I don't believe you." But his face was twitching, and I knew he *did* believe me. I twisted the knife. "Call the Vortex Chamber. Ask them."

He did. I could not hear what they told him on the telephone. But I knew what the general content of the message had to be.

"It is so," he said thoughtfully. "Very well, then, the woman may leave with you." His face on the screen nodded to a guard, who then went into an adjoining room. "How do I know you won't release the Vortex suddenly after you leave here?" he asked.

"Basically, you don't. On the other hand, I would be a fool to destabilize your Vortex while I am still underground. I would risk a quake before I could get out. And as I pass to the outside, my control becomes weaker, because it is subject to the inverse square law of electromagnetic radiation."

"Why should we believe that?" he murmured.

"And finally," I continued, ignoring him, "I have given you my word. Return Beatra to me unharmed, with a safe conduct to the surface, and we will leave you and your city unharmed. And there is a curious irony, Mr. President, that even if I do not trust you, you do trust me."

He was silent a moment; then he shrugged. "Very well. I suppose I will never know whether you could truly harm the Vortex. But I accept the possibility that you might. You may go, and take the woman. She will be out in a moment, and you and she and the animal will be escorted to one of the regular police floaters in the parking area. You can drive it out, the same way you came in."

Even though I could not get into his mind during any of this, I knew that he thought in the end it would make no difference. As far as he understood the situation, Beatra and I would be dead of the poison in a matter of hours.

They brought her out.

My mind was in hers even before I saw her. She was unconscious, apparently heavily sedated. But images of terror and pain still beat chaotically within the confines of her cerebrum, running to and fro like frightened forest creatures trying to escape a fire. Horrid things had been done to her. Before they wheeled her out on the little cot, I knew this. And a part of me knew exactly what they had done, but it was a dread knowledge buried in my subconscious, and to protect my sanity I could not permit it to come forth into my present waking knowledge.

She was accompanied by a man in a long white gown. I was in his mind too. He said, "She is presently resting. She will be fine as soon as the sleeping potion wears away." He lied.

I now bent over her. It had to be done. I studied those once perfect lips. I saw the tiny bloody holes that minutes before had held the sutures that bound her lips together. Very gently I squeezed down the lower jaw and looked into the oral cavity. It was nearly empty. The tongue had been cut out.

I knew what had happened to her. They had done it to the Returner, and now to her. They had given to her the Vow of Silence.

It struck me now that I knew the identity of the

Returner. I knew the floater, wrecked and burnt in the grotto. My mind did now what it had resolutely refused to do these past twenty-odd hours: it admitted that it recognized the charred figurehead on the prow of that floater. It was a wolfhead.

And that voiceless Father Phaedrus, that mad, withered monk who had given me such vivid mental images, taken, they said, from the Returner. Phaedrus had tried to tell me a great thing, and I was too dense to grasp it. ("You have understood very little," he had chided me.) Ah, small wonder he had been able to transmit such clear and crystalline pictures from the Returner's broken mind. Yes, there was the thing my grandfather knew, and the Brothers knew, and that no one had dared tell me: the ravaged Returner and the shattered Father Phaedrus were one and the same man, namely, my father.

Once again, I saw him in the floater, escaping downriver. Where had he gotten the floater? He may have stolen it. They may even have thrown him into it, and turned it loose over the river, for sport. No matter. I rode with him, through the forest of stone pillars, over the falls, and down the canyon, and then, somewhere, down the next, and greatest, and final sickening fall, far, far below until the helpless little craft was thrown with all the waters of Lethe into the molten earth cleft. Through all this, the staunch walls and thick transparent hood must have remained intact. And it would seem that the floater had not itself touched the surface of the molten rock. He had piloted well. And now the journey upward, in the middle of a column of superheated steam. Then he was through, and out, and stumbling from his smoking craft, and collapsing on the long snow dune.

To him, my father, they had done this.

And now my wife.

From the visibox the President studied me with cold eyes. His face was totally without expression.

Something was happening inside my brain. I was losing control. I remember thinking, after all this time, I can't slip now. But it did no good. Things were slipping away.

I began to tremble. My teeth chattered and I remember listening to a curious rattling sound: it was the knocking of my knees.

Then something like lightning struck me. Time stopped. I was paralyzed.

When time began to flow again, I knew I had done a colossal thing. And the consequences I understood very well.

My vortical powers were gone. I was still able to enter minds, but I no longer had the power to make a ball of light, or to do anything that drew on the power of the great Vortex.

What had happened?

I knew.

The thing that I knew was this: I had done something terrible to the Vortex. At the moment, I felt a certain detachment about what I had done. I found myself discussing the situation dispassionately with myself. Had I knocked it off its axis? Was it now spinning off-center like a gyrating top in its last throes, with the Keepers desperately trying to restabilize it? No, what I had done was much worse than that. The thing that I had done, and the reason I had lost my vortical powers, was that—in my murderous emotional reaction—*I had moved the Vortex out of its chamber altogether!* And where was it now? In the river alongside the entrance to the Vortex Chamber, and very likely inundating the dock area with crashing waters cast up in its dying agony. In seconds even this greatest of machines must yield to the force of the torrent and be swept and tumbled to the waiting maw of the great chute that led down to the molten magma. After it had its assignation with Hades, it would be blown out through the Spume, broken, shattered, a great puzzle to all who would see it in future generations.

But the President did not know any of this. Not yet. He did not know that he could kill me immediately and with impunity. Nor was I inclined to enlighten him. He would understand all too soon.

I had to get Beatra out of here.

I grabbed the front handle on the wheeled stretcher and pulled it toward the waiting floater. Virgil followed close behind.

Someone was calling to the President. He turned away.

The walkway was shuddering under my feet as I slammed the vessel door shut. There was an odd haze in the air. Dust began to swirl around the machine. The automatic windshield jets came on and washed the glass area clean. I looked up. Flakes of rock were filtering down from the street ceiling. There were a couple of clicks as bigger pieces hit the floater hood. The foreshocks had begun. Fortunately the floater's transparent panels were thick, and apparently were hermetically sealed. But I was concerned about Beatra. I did not want her to get bounced about. I looked around the cabin interior hurriedly. There was a bench on one side, complete with straps, probably for prisoner control. I quickly transferred Beatra to it, prone, and strapped her in as best I could. I tossed the stretcher out.

As I pulled away, I looked behind me.

A dozen guards were running to the line of floaters waiting in the vehicle area. Evidently the Keepers had already notified the President. But why should he care about me now? I thought it strange. This man put revenge above the salvation of his country. He should be formulating plans to deal with the great quakes that would soon be racking these streets. I could imagine his thought processes: they must be a jumble. True, he must know the earthquake was coming. Ah, he must want very much to take a floater full of henchmen and escape to the surface. But he probably felt trapped, because he thought the space capsule had already emptied its death canister, and the contents would be reaching the earth's surface within hours. And so he told himself, if *he* had to die, I, the invader, had to die too, and first.

Even now, at this very late stage, I would have been glad to tell him he had nothing to fear on the surface, and that he still had time to save some of his people. I did not suppose that all of the undergrounders were cruel and savage, for I had met the colonel, and I knew there were many good people here. But it was futile even to think about it.

Our floater got a considerable start on our pursuers, but they had special pursuit vessels, and they were gaining on us. Also, the bow gun of the foremost vessel began firing. I immediately began to zigzag my ship. It made me lose precious time, but I could not risk damage to the ship or to Beatra at this stage, especially since I could now see the entrance to the colonel's secret exit passage half a mile ahead.

I thought once of forming a light-ball to blind my pursuers. And then I remembered. I couldn't form a light-ball. My vortectic powers had vanished with the Vortex sphere.

I stole a look at Beatra. She was still unconscious, and now she was beginning to breathe in guttural gasps. A drop of blood had trickled down the side of her mouth. I had to get her to the Brothers. She was dying. I controlled my thoughts and tried to concentrate on the next half-mile.

It was going to be very dark in the old, water-hewn passages. I fished around in the compartment under the dashboard for the portolamp. I never found it.

There was an explosion overhead. Great hunks of the street ceiling crashed down on the roof of the floater. They were firing accurately, and it was going to be very close.

Just then something flashed in the middle of the

street, not far ahead of us, and another explosion
rocked the floater.

I peered forward, unbelieving. A trio of police
floaters were approaching swiftly from the front. The
President had radioed ahead for reinforcements. We
would never reach the colonel's secret passage.

Death lay ahead, and death lay behind.

We were trapped.

Why were they doing this? What difference did it
make to them? I quickly probed the mind of the driver
of the lead vessel. I got a shock. The President!
Somehow, I had thought he was far behind. But no. He
was up front and had assumed personal control of my
pursuit. Well, if he wanted the trophy of the hunt, he
would have to earn it. He had the advantage of
knowledge of the terrain, but I had the advantage of
desperation. I could elude him. I had to believe it.

Here was an intersection. Do I turn right or left?

I knew already. It would be to the left. I knew from
the memory wisp of the map in the guardhouse that if I
turned left I would come to a descender. The descender
would take me down a number of levels. To what? I
didn't know for sure, but I could guess. What was the
bottom layer to this doomed city?

The river.

Our floater was already around the bend and diving
nose first into the descender. The air whistled past the
floater skin as it screamed down. We were still in the
descender shaft when the first shell struck the bottom
of the shaft with a blinding crash. And this was
fortunate, because neither Virgil's eyes nor my
headlights showed the terminus clearly. I arced up just
in time, headed down the only exit. My tail skid
actually brushed a piece of rubble on the descender
bottom.

Would I now crash into some dank dead end, or
would I find the river? And what difference would it
make? For the river led but to the Spume, and Beatra

would never survive that dread journey. I looked down at her white face. I detected no movement beneath the bonds that held her to the side bench. Did she still live? I could not stop to find out.

There was a sudden great booming behind me. Something back there was collapsing. Another severe temblor. I wondered whether it had caught any of my pursuers. I stole a look at the rearview mirror. There were a pair of lights moving back there. That meant at least one floater. The President? Probably. He alone would be this persistent, determined that my death should precede his.

"Watch it!" cried Virgil into my mind.

I dodged something big in the middle of my path.

A stone pillar!

I was over the river.

Another left turn, and I was threading the pillars and moving downstream.

Was this victory? Yes, indeed! As long as we lived, we were winners. If we strung out life another five minutes, we had at least won the five-minute prize.

Something exploded on my right. My pursuer was still shooting. It had to be the President. A trained guard would have been a much better marksman. Nevertheless, I took no chances. I weaved from one side of the river to the other, trying to keep as many pillars between me and my enemy as possible.

And now things were happening to the cavern roof. Every few seconds a piece would fall into the river. I could hear splashes around me even through the thick panels of the floater, and the headbeams picked up several disturbances in the waters ahead. By some miracle, nothing struck us. I actually felt in more danger from these dislodged stones than I did from the following floater, for there was no evasive action I could take from them.

Another long, horrible boom off to one side. Then several crashes that came right through the hermetically sealed walls of my vessel. The end was coming.

We had passed the shaft area where, hours ago, Virgil and I had fallen into the river, and now we approached the falls.

What had happened to the pursuer? I had detected no sign of him for a mile. But no matter. We had other concerns. The temblors were now bringing down bigger and bigger sections of the arching ceiling, and stalactites, stalagmites, and stone pillars were being snapped and hurled about like sticks.

At that moment I noticed lights again in my rearview mirror. It was he. I could not see his craft, but I knew.

And then the light was very suddenly snuffed out. Almost immediately a rolling boom shook my ship. The roof had fallen in on him, and it was still falling. I was glad. He deserved it. But if I were not to join him, I would have to hurry on.

We passed the dock of the Vortex Chamber. Even without shining my headbeams directly on it, I could see the great three-hundred-foot hole in the Chamber wall where the Vortex had burst through on its way into the canyon. My handiwork, but I had no time to admire it, and no time to speculate about the ultimate fate of the great sphere.

I ventured a look down at my wife. It was too dark to see her. I peeked into her mind. She still lived.

On we sped down the chasm. Walls, channel, ceiling were falling, cracking away, collapsing all around us. It was miraculous that our little ship had not been hit. For the moment it led a charmed life, but that couldn't last. Our only hope to escape immediate death was to accept the deferred death of the Spume: down, down, falling with the river into the hell-hot gut of the earth, and then tossed up again within the column of steam. Down one leg of the V, then up the other.

Faster and faster, slanting down, down. There was a sickening feeling in my stomach. Virgil whimpered.

But there was no retreat. Behind us, a world was dissolving.

We struck the torrent. The ship went under water. There were a few trickles inside, but generally the water-seals held.

Still down, down, with the irresistible flood.

In a moment the ship would hit bottom, possibly even touch a sea of red-hot flowing magma—and that would be the end.

But the ship touched nothing. It paused, stopped dead in the water, and seemed to hang momentarily in liquid space. In *liquid* water. There was no steam. It wasn't even warm.

And now we were rising again. Slowly at first, then faster and faster, like a bubble in water.

Were we coming back up into the river? No. Nothing so simple. We were truly rising in the other leg of the V. How could this be? What had happened to the magma? Evidently something had plugged the bottom of the V so that the water could not contact the hot liquid rock. And I knew what it must be—what was serving to insulate the river from that submerged lava. The thing that had plugged the great hole was the Vortex sphere. But it couldn't last. The heat must soon melt the sphere shell, and after that the waters would strike the magma once more. And the entire water plug in my arm of the V would be blown up into the skies with volcanic violence—with my floater riding on top of it like a cork.

But we had a chance.

The floater had by now risen to the top of the water column. It bumped into the walls of the Spume shaft from time to time, but not violently enough to break the windows. There was a lot of water in the cabin floor, but even so the leaks were small and the seals held pretty well.

The waters had stopped rising. Perhaps we had reached the level of the river, and this was as high up the Spume channel as we would be carried.

I peered upward through the overhead portal but I could see nothing. I had hoped to see a tiny piece of sky, but either it was still night outside or else the channel made a bend that shut out a view of the heavens. No matter. We had to get out of here. The Spume would reactivate at any moment.

I turned the ascension control lever. The ship didn't budge an inch. I turned it back and forth a couple of times. No luck. The mechanism was probably waterlogged. I had just about given up when we began to move. But then I noted that we hadn't left the water surface. We were moving because the water column was moving. The Vortex sphere had evidently broken up and no longer served to insulate the waters of Lethe from the magmas within the earth. The bottom of the V was unplugged. Far below us vast and instant quantities of steam had been made, and we were being shot out of the Spume muzzle, like the lead ball in an ancient gunpowder rifle.

Virgil and I were thrown to the floor of the cabin and pinned there as though by a great flattening hand.

Up and up we went, faster and faster. A couple of times the little vessel bounced off the channel walls, and I thought we were done for.

We burst through the mouth of the Spume crater at an unimaginable velocity. And we were soaring, and beginning to decelerate. I was able to crawl to the controls. I actually had time to look out, and down, over the Spume-stricken wasteland. None of the control levers responded to my frantic tests. Everything was shorted or jammed. We reached the apex of our flight parabola at about two miles, and now we began to fall.

Beatra, I thought, you will never awaken. But at least there will be no pain.

How long does it take to fall two miles? The Brothers have a mathematical formula to make this calculation. I have never worked it out. All I remember is, in the beginning it seemed to stretch out forever, but in the end it seemed to be almost instantaneous. I knelt by Beatra and held her hands. They were icy.

And then we crashed, and I blacked out.

The next thing I remember, I was carrying her out of the floater, and skidding and sliding down to the bottom of a soft white hill, where Virgil already awaited us.

We had fallen into the side of the Spume's snow dune, which, despite the fact that it was early summer, was still largely unmelted. The soft snow had saved our lives.

"How is she?" asked Virgil.

"She's in bad shape. How bad, I don't know. We have to get help."

Several body-sized boulders fell in a cluster not a dozen feet from us. The Spume was now beginning to discharge an accumulated burden of debris swept into it by the river.

"We have to get out of here," I said. "Make for the hill."

Beneath us the earth shook and shuddered. More temblors. We hurried on up to the crest of the hill. And it wasn't just the Spume ejecta that we had to worry about. The underground quakes would soon strike the surface with equal fury. At any moment there might be landslides that would carry us back down to the very mouth of the reactivated Spume.

In the near dark we began the toiling ascent to the rim of the hill. Several times rock avalanches swept down on their side of us. But we finally got to the top without being hit.

Only a few of the brighter stars were still visible. There was a definite dark blue tint in the skies. Dawn was well on its way, and the sun would be up in half an hour.

But we were still not secure. Clutching Beatra to my

body as best I could, I stumbled down the other side of the hill. We were halfway to the valley when I looked down in the dim dawn light and saw the earth moving. Giant ripples were advancing across the surface of the land. It was like watching the sea. They were leisurely waves, perhaps a hundred yards from crest to crest, and eight to ten feet high. As they came on, I could see what they were doing to the trees. At first, the tree tops would seem to move majestically with the advancing wave-front, leaning at first to the front, then to the rear, and then, within a few seconds, a great many of the individual trees seemed simply to pop out of the ground. There they lay, stricken and broken.

A great cloud of dust was stirred up by these surface waves, mercifully blotting out the destruction that was left behind.

Virgil whimpered and pressed against my leg.

And then the earth was moving under us. We were all thrown to the ground. I sensed that the disturbances moved rapidly on up the hill behind us.

And then, save for a prolonged, fading roar and the hanging dust, it was over.

I looked up toward the hill crest. It was gone. The whole hill was gone. Everything there was as level as our fields and meadows back home.

It was easy to visualize what had happened underground. If anyone had survived the series of preliminary temblors, this big quake would have crushed him before he could have moved ten yards. Very few of them could have suffered very long. Some—living and dead—were perhaps swept into the great river, and would emerge hours later in the Spume as unrecognizable bits of broken bone and thoroughly cooked flesh. The carrion creatures would feast for days about the Spume cone.

I had destroyed a three-thousand-year dream.

"God pity them," I whispered. But it was hard to feel anything.

I picked up Beatra and the three of us headed down the valley where I hoped I would find the colonel's party. I was certain he had had the wit to take his group up in their floater as soon as the first intimations of the quake reached them. I could take one of his ships and get Beatra to the Brothers in New Bollamer.

I smiled grimly. Just as the Brothers had predicted, *their* vortectic powers were gone now, too, and they couldn't have the faintest idea why.

After a few hundred yards I had to rest. I laid my wife down gently on a patch of mossy turf. She looked strangely at peace, as though the events of the past weeks and the last hours were a total fabrication conjured up in my mind alone. Her eyes were closed as if in soft sleep.

I just stood there, in a numb stupor, looking down at her.

Virgil threw back her head and began to howl.

Epilog

As I FINISH these pages I hear the cries of wild geese overhead. For three nights running, I have heard them. I must lay down my pen, for these signs of spring overwhelm me. I must step outdoors, upon the rough porch of my cabin, and then out into the patch I have shoveled out of the winter snows, and look to the skies.

It is early April, and my lungs and heart fill with wonder at the beauty of the night, and of this place.

But back to my history.

How did it all end? That is perhaps the wrong question.

Parts of New Bollamer and some of the nearby villages were pretty well shattered by the series of great quakes of that last hour, now so long ago, but these places have long since been rebuilt, better than ever. Our manor was not touched, nor was Grandfather or his shops. I think he still lives, but I am not sure. I never go into the villages anymore.

Colonel Aksel and his handful of technicians got out just before the main quake. They were quickly welcomed and absorbed into the factories of New Bollamer. Within a decade they advanced our technology a century. And all this despite a certain weakness of the eyes. I understand they now number among the richest and most influential of our citizenry. These men represented the last traces of Dis, a place now gone after a grim and static history of thirty centuries. Is anyone still down there? Did anyone escape the temblors and quakes? I think it doubtful, but actually, I think we will never know for sure. All entrances have been long collapsed, and there is no longer any access to the city. I do not want to know. It is all part of a nightmare that I want to forget.

In that last hour, on what was once a hillside, Virgil and I parted. I said to her, "Go north and west, into Vania, Nyock, Canda. You were once a hunter. You can hunt again. The woods are full of game. Rabbits, deer. Find a wolf-pack. Some old lobo will think you're the prettiest thing that ever came down the trail. Raise a family."

"Yes," she said agreeably, "I will indeed be a hunter. Of men. And my cubs will hunt men, for I will teach them. I have found the human liver to be a rare delicacy. And I have found his heart, preferably still struggling to pump blood, a gourmet's delight. Ah yes, I have tasted his blood, and I can read his mind. I will hunt him easily. He will learn to fear me."

"Well, Miss *loup garou*, just don't get yourself shot."

"*Loup garou?* Yes, that's it. Werewolf. I have the body of a wolf, but I am not a wolf. I have part of your mind, but I am not you, not a human being. And that's because of what you have done to me. I have an insert from a male human mind in the body of a female wolf. Am I male or female? Am I wolf or human? It is not good to die, not knowing who you are, and with your last thoughts overlain with perplexing ambiguities. Goodbye, Jeremy."

Without a backward look she bounded away and disappeared into the scrub. Have I seen her since? Sometimes I think so.

Beginning at this little clearing the hillock sweeps up to a summit. It is on that ridge that I think I sometimes see Virgil. She never comes any closer. But on a cold and frosty morning, when the chill makes a fog of my breath, I might see her head silhouetted against the gray sky.

I come now to the gentle mound of earth. There is no stone to mark it, and it is brown and desolate under its patches of snow. But as spring comes on it will soon be ringed about with crocuses and daffodils. And then will come the scent of wild cherry pollen, even though there are no wild cherry trees anywhere in the forest hereabouts.

Laughter by a Waterfall
One evening late I wandered here
To sit and watch the pounding foam
And then I thought I heard you call
Too late I whirled. For you were gone.

Hair Tossed in the Wind
Where have gone those golden strands
That worked a glamor on the air
And caressed the fingers of my hands
As oft I touched those cheeks so fair.

Snowflakes on a Grave
At morning when the sun is low
When dark blue shadows laced with light
Attend me in my walk,
I hear the rippling river flow,
I hear the limp-top hemlocks sigh
And on this mound the snowflakes knock
But there is no answer.

SCIENCE FICTION BESTSELLERS
FROM BERKLEY

Frank Herbert

DUNE   (03698-7—$2.25)

DUNE MESSIAH   (03585-9—$1.75)

CHILDREN OF DUNE   (03310-4—$1.95)

Philip José Farmer

THE FABULOUS RIVERBOAT   (03378-3—$1.50)

NIGHT OF LIGHT   (03366-X—$1.50)

TO YOUR SCATTERED
BODIES GO   (03175-6—$1.75)

* * * * * * *